About the book:

"If angels wear Vicki's and the devil wears Prada, I guess I was a taste of heaven & hell back then, because King had completely turned daddy's little angel into a hell of a rider..."

My name is Kennedy Desiree Carter. I met the love of my life, Damion "King" Carter, five years ago. Back then, you would not have been able to convince me of the way that he would change my life, in good ways and bad. I was a good girl; on my way to college with a high GPA and big dreams of becoming a Child Psychologist. Yet, as soon as I met King, I also dreamed of being the best rider that any street nigga had ever seen. I was a good girl with a bad boy fetish, and King was the ultimate bad boy that came to love me in ways that I had never felt before. They say ride or die is the highest level of loyalty that you will find in a person, and King had found that in me; even though it eventually meant my own suffering. Yet, the suffering never fazed me because I knew that we loved each other. Some would say too much, and I couldn't argue with that because loving him sent me to a place that I thought I would never be, all because he put his trust in the wrong people.

Every dope boy needs to realize that sometimes the realest person on his team is his girl, and King found that out the hard way.

D1519603

About the author:

Jessica N. Watkins was born April 1st in Chicago, Illinois. She obtained a Bachelors of Arts with Focus in Psychology from DePaul University and Masters of Applied Professional Studies with focus in Business Administration from the like institution. Working in Hospital Administration for the majority of her career, Watkins has also been an author of fiction literature since the young age of nine. Eventually she used writing as an outlet during her freshmen year of high school as a single parent: "In the third grade I entered a short story contest with a fiction tale of an apple tree that refused to grow despite the efforts of the darling main character. My writing evolved from apple trees to my seventh and eighth grade classmates paying me to read novels I wrote about kids our age living the lives our parents wouldn't dare let us". At the age of twenty-eight, Watkins' chronicles have matured into steamy, humorous, and realistic tales of African American Romance and Urban Fiction.

In September 2013, Jessica's most recent novel, Secrets of a Side Bitch, published by SBR Publications, reached #1 on multiple charts. Jessica N. Watkins is available for talks, workshops or book signings. Email her for more information at jessica@femistrypress.net.

DAVID WEAVER PRESENTS

A THUG'S LOVE

JESSICA N. WATKINS

Release day...

Chapter One

Jada

It was May 13, 2015. Finally, the temperature had risen above sixty degrees, and the sun was shining. It was a beautiful day. Not only because of the weather but because my cousin, Kennedy, was getting out of prison.

"Here she comes!" As soon as I heard Siren's excited squeal from the back seat, I tore my eyes away from Instagram and looked out of the windshield of my Range Rover. Once my eyes landed on her, a smile spread across my face, realizing that it was real. King's queen was finally free.

Kennedy was walking slowly and timidly down the steps of Logan Correctional Center in Lincoln, Illinois. Her nervousness came off as if she was grasping the reality that she was actually leaving the place she had spent the last three years. Laying eyes on her was more than a breath of fresh air, and surprisingly, she looked better than she had before she'd gotten locked up. She looked like an improved version of herself. Her long, natural ponytail was far from the eighteen-inch weave she was used to rocking, and her bare face was clear and free of blemishes since she hadn't been exposed to all of the makeup and harsh chemicals that would have normally broken her out. The lack of fatty foods and no recreation except exercise had given her once full-figure tight curves that I knew King was going to go crazy over. As Kennedy walked toward us holding a bag of "parting gifts" from the prison, she tried to appear cool. But I knew that she was just as excited as me and Siren were that she was finally coming home.

Frantically, I blew the horn and rolled down the window, shouting, "Somebody play the horns and trumpets! Here comes the queen!"

As soon as she heard my voice, Kennedy tried to hold back a smile that I'd managed to see beyond the anxiousness of finally being free.

"Come on, Siren, let's get out." As I climbed out, Siren took Kennedy's daughter, Kayla, out of her car seat. Kayla began to whine and fuss, and the sound of her baby's voice broke all of Kennedy's cool. Her once laid-back swagger shattered into a loud weep, instant tears, and a sprint toward us.

Siren and I ran toward her with smiles so big that our cheeks were hurting.

"Heeey!" I squealed with open arms, ready to hug my girl for the first time in years. "Oh my God!"

"Girl, I can't believe it," Siren exhaled. "Finally!"

But Kennedy wasn't even listening to us as we all collided in a group hug. She tore her daughter from Siren's arms and broke down in tears as she laid kisses all over her face. Kayla was squirming to get away, and the only sound surrounding our huddle was the cries of a mother that had been longing to hold her daughter again. My heart broke for them both because it was obvious that Kayla had forgotten who her mother was since she was only four months when Kennedy was arrested. But my cousin was so wrapped up in seeing her child for the first time in years that she didn't notice Kayla's frustration. Kennedy hadn't seen her daughter since she'd started her sentence because she had refused to let us bring Kayla to a prison. Kennedy's sobs brought tears to mine and Siren's eyes.

It was a few moments later when Kennedy finally decided to pay Siren and me some attention. Still holding a fussing Kayla in her arms, she took turns wrapping an arm around each of us as happy tears of relief streamed down her face. Siren and I had visited the prison many times, so those tears weren't just because she was finally able to see us, but I was sure that she was relieved that she was now seeing us on *this* side of the prison gates.

"C'mon. Let's get this drive out of the way," I told Kennedy, as we walked toward my truck, still holding each other. "King is blowing my phone up. You know he can't wait to see you."

I saw a bashful smile spread across Kennedy's face as I walked over to the driver's side. "I can't wait to see him either, but I want to get out of this fucking jumpsuit and get rid of this gawd damn ponytail! I've been so tired of him seeing me looking this way. That's why I didn't want him to pick me up. Now that I'm out, the first time that he sees me, I want to be *cute*."

Siren sucked her teeth as she climbed into the passenger side, and Kennedy got into the backseat with Kayla. "Girl, you could have walked out of there with your hair all over your head and King would *not* have cared."

"I know, but for the last three years I always envisioned that once I was free, and we saw each other, I would be as beautiful as I was before I got locked up. Did y'all make my appointment?"

"Yes, of course," Siren answered.

King was making sure that on Kennedy's first day out she was truly being treated like a queen. The plan was that she would spend her day with us girls, being primped and pampered for the welcome home party which King had been planning for a whole year. And like a true queen, at the party, she would be presented, appearing as perfect and pretty as royalty, to her King, for the first time in three years.

"I want some of that Indonesian shit y'all wearin'," Kennedy said as she ran her fingers through Siren's bone-straight twenty-eight inches.

As Siren and I broke out in giggles, I started the engine and asked Kennedy, "Indonesian? You mean *Brazilian*?"

"Yeah, *that*."

Before I could crack a joke about how the time she'd missed on the outside had left her totally ignorant of what was poppin', the phone on the console began to ring. It was the phone that King had given me for Kennedy, and the motherfucka wasn't even patient enough to wait for my text message telling him that she was out.

Immediately, I grabbed it and handed it to her. "Here, Kennedy. That's your phone ... and your King."

I quickly glanced in the rearview mirror to catch the smile on her face before she answered with the cutest, girliest voice I'd ever heard. "Hey, baby."

I couldn't hear what King was saying, but I could imagine.

KING

"Hey, baby."

Thugs ain't supposed to cry, and in twenty-nine years of being on this earth, I had only cried a few times in my adult life, and each one of those times had something to do with Kennedy and our daughter, Kayla. When Kayla was born, I bawled seeing her for the first time, and then when Kennedy was locked up. Now tears were pooling at my eyelids, and I allowed one or two of them to fall before wiping them away because, despite my manhood, the tears were falling for a good cause. I was finally hearing my queen's voice on this side of those prison walls, and I knew that I would finally be able to touch her again soon.

"How are you?" Kennedy asked me. And that's how my baby was. No matter her circumstances, she was first and foremost concerned about me. She was eight years younger, but she always took care of me like the mother I didn't have, even while she was locked up.

"Don't worry about me," I told her. "I should be asking you that."

She sighed real heavy. "I'm happy. I can't wait to see you."

My voice dropped to a tone that I knew would make her panties wet. "You know I can't wait to see you." And that was the motherfuckin' truth. I hadn't been able to lay hands on my beau in three years, and I had a lot of catching up to do.

"You better stop. We aren't going to make that party if you keep talking to me like that."

"Baby, we can say fuck that party altogether." I chuckled, but I was dead serious. "Just give me the word."

She giggled. "No, King. You spent so much money on it. We *have* to go. Everybody is looking forward to it… But we can leave early."

A lustful grin spread across my face. "Bet, baby. I–"

"Umm, tell King that he can talk to you later," I heard Jada say. "We have gossiping to do."

"Go ahead, baby, and kick it with your girls."

"*Nooo*," Kennedy whined. "I miss you."

"I know. But let them have a couple hours with you because as soon as you get to me, you're all mine. And I'm not letting go."

There was a slight pause. I imagined her pussy creaming in response to my words. My dick grew rock hard as I lay on my California King. I *couldn't wait* to get in that pussy.

"Okay, baby. See you later."

"I can't wait. I love you more than anything," I told her.

"I love you more than Kanye loves Kanye."

We both laughed and said goodbye before hanging up.

I took a deep breath before getting out of the bed. Kennedy being out of the pen was unreal. The last few years without my baby had felt like thirty. For thirty-six long months, I had lived with a serious craving for her in my heart, along with guilt. I was her man, her king. I was supposed to have protected her from my lifestyle. Instead, she ended up in prison because of my bullshit. To this day, I didn't know how she had gotten caught up, who had set her up, or why. The day that she got arrested was an ordinary day. It was routine, but I knew that I shouldn't have let her go. Though she had never made a run for me before that night, she had followed my instructions to the letter. However, she was pulled over and caught with over twenty bricks of cocaine. My workers had those bricks hidden from eagle's eyes, but as Kennedy had told it, the detectives that stopped her went straight to every hiding place in the Jeep Cherokee that she was driving.

Each day that she spent away, I felt like less of a man for not finding the motherfucka who had set her up and making him pay for taking away years of me and my baby's lives. My crew and I had whooped a lot of ass trying to figure it out, but at the end of the day, none of our opps or even our friends had proven guilty.

I hadn't been living since Kennedy was locked up, only existing. I had been a walking shell, a man with no soul, but because I had nothing else to commit myself to, business had tripled. I now had a house for her that was three times bigger than the one we had when she left. She already had a walk-in closet waiting for her that was full of Chanel, Herves Ledger, Christian Louboutin, Giuseppe, and even those bandage dresses from the boutiques on Instagram that all the females were coppin'. I had even set up a day of pampering for her before her welcome home party. She would walk into the Shrine nightclub with her makeup done, fresh hairdo, new outfit, and relaxed from a full body massage at Mario Tricoci.

I didn't require all of that. She could have come home to me in her prison jumpsuit for all I gave a damn, but she insisted on being dolled up when she saw me for the first time once she was free. And as always, Kennedy's wish was my command.

Release day...

CHAPTER TWO

KENNEDY

Pulling up in front of the Shrine nightclub in the passenger seat of King's Phantom Rolls Royce felt like a dream. I had spent three years in a dingy jumpsuit while lying in a dirty, small, gray, concrete cell. Now, I was in a blacked out luxury vehicle in an all-white Herves Ledger bandage dress with hair that fell so softly down my back that it felt like silk. My day of pampering and cuddling with a feisty Kayla was exactly what I needed after being locked up with dirty bitches as I lay on a hard cot. However, every minute I spent getting pampered, I impatiently waited for it to be over so that I could see my King. As the valet opened the passenger side door, my body knew that the moment that I was reunited with King was in my very near future. I felt tingles all over. Sure, King had visited me, but he hadn't been able to touch me, to kiss me, and ... *shit*... I could *not* wait.

A few guys standing in line made obscene remarks as I waited for Jada and Siren to meet me at the curb.

"*Shaaat*, baby! That ass phat as *hell*!"

"Let me see what that booty do, ma!"

Clearly these young boys didn't know who I was. King had rented the entire club out for the night, so everyone in attendance knew that this was a welcome home party for King's wife. If they knew that I was Mrs. Damion "King" Carter, these young bucks would be too scared of King's wrath to be so ignorant. But I simply rolled my eyes, and I decided to spare their lives by shrugging it off and not telling King of their immature antics. Yet, I appreciated the confirmation that I was looking good. When I'd gotten locked up, I had just given birth to Kayla. On top of the fact that I was kind of a big girl anyway, the baby weight had me extra chunky. At 5'5", the two-hundred and fifteen pounds was not sitting well on me at all. Let King tell it, I was thick as hell, and he loved that my waist was small, but I hated that I had to wear spanks with every fucking thing. Though being locked up was no walk in the park, besides reading, I did spend a lot of time walking and working out in the yard. It also helped that the only food I trusted was the rice, fish, and fruit. Therefore, I had contoured my body into a figure that I liked seeing in the mirror. I was still a plus-size chick. I had purposely kept my curves because King loved them. Only now, I didn't need Spanx or those waist cinchers that Jada and Siren had told me about. When I slipped on the bandage dress and white

13

Red Bottoms, I damn sure liked what I saw in the mirror, but I was nervous because I hadn't been out in the public for years.

Jada and Siren were looking flawless in all white as well. They had also gotten pampered that day. Their boyfriends, Dolla and Meech, who were also King's right hand men, had made sure that Jada and Siren received the same services as I had so that we all would look perfect when we walked into my welcome home party. And that's exactly what happened; when we walked in the club, we received smiles and nods of approval and confirmation that we looked just as good as we felt. All eyes were on us. We looked exactly how we were expected to look, and our appearances spoke volumes: we were the women of three of the biggest hustlers in Chicago. A lot of people in the crowd greeted me as I fought to get to where King told me he would be. A lot of people from our hood were very excited to see me, and I was excited to see them. But, unfortunately, my focus was on my man, who I finally laid eyes on when I noticed that he was standing on the stage in VIP, watching me with the most loving eyes and adoring smile on his face.

I didn't think it was possible for King to look better, but in that all-white suit, he looked like my ghetto angel. He was wearing a custom-made suit that fit his body like a comfortable glove. My man was a big guy, standing 6'4" and weighing nearly two-hundred and ninety pounds, but it was all toned. He had shoulders like Dwight Howard, crowning a body like Reggie Bush.

He was dark like both of them too, with a chiseled face, and soft eyes that gave him a GQ, modelesque look. Yet, he had a cold stare and so many tattoos that he was far more intimidating than any model. Before I got locked up, King was rocking long dreads. But a month into my sentence, he'd cut them off and into a fade with an afro top that brought out the sharp features in his face. It gave him mature sex appeal too.

I nearly knocked people down trying to get to that stage as the music changed, and the crowd went up in hysterics.

♪ I'm like, "Hey, what's up? Hello."
Seen your pretty ass soon as you came in that door.
I just wanna chill. Got a sack for us to roll.
Married to the money. Introduced her to my stove.
Showed her how to whip it, now she remixin' for low.
She my trap queen, let her hit the bando.
We be countin' up, watch how far them bands go.
We just set a goal, talkin' matchin' Lambos.
A 50, 60 grand, five hundred grams though.
Man, I swear I love her, how she work the damn pole.
Hit the strip club, we be letting bands go.
Everybody hating, we just call them fans though.
In love with the money, I ain't ever letting go! ♪

Girls were popping their asses and guys were doing dances that were foreign to me. I pushed past them all to the point that a bouncer pushed his way through the crowd to assist me. But when we got to the staircase that led to the stage, I no longer needed the bouncer's help. I nearly took flight as tears came to my eyes. Ordinarily, I would have hated that I was about to mess up my perfectly beat face with my tears, but tonight I didn't give a fuck. I was home, and my King was about to be within my arm's reach.

I had waited for this moment for three years...one hundred and fifty-three weeks...one-thousand and seventy-one days. I didn't give a damn about this MAC makeup or Red Bottoms. I ran to King, and the entire club cheered and screamed for us as I fell into his arms. I had imagined what I would say when I was in arms again. It was going to be perfect, and sexy, and sultry... but I couldn't say shit!

My heart melted when he grabbed my face and said, "Hey, baby."

I couldn't find the rehearsed words that I had repeated in my mind over and over again on the way there, so I just kissed him, which was what I had been waiting to do for so long. Again, I could hear the crowd cheering for us over the music as he sucked my tongue and lips. I melted into that man's arms and sucked his face as if no one else was there but us.

"Damn, I missed you," he breathed through our kisses, and I could only moan in response. "Baby, we gotta stop before I fuck you in front of all these people."

I smiled, reluctantly left his mouth, and looked into his eyes. Words finally came to me. "I missed you so much," left my lips in disbelief as I couldn't take my teary eyes off of him. "I love you *so* much."

He lustfully bit the corner of his bottom lip as he promised, "I love you too, baby."

We smiled at each other as if we were meeting for the first time. Suddenly, a crowd surrounded me. I looked around and screamed when I saw Dolla, Meech, and other members of King's entourage. Their smiles were so bright as they hugged me, danced with me and King, and welcomed me home.

King wrapped his arms around me and began to dance as well as the music returned to my ears. "This is my shit!"

King chuckled into my ear. "I know. That's why I told them to play it when you walked in. Plus you're my *queen*, baby."

I smiled as everyone around me rapped along to the lyrics, "*Married to the money, introduced her to my stove. Showed her how to whip it, now she remixin' for low. She my trap queen...* " They all moved in dances that I didn't know. But I still knew *how* to dance, so... I danced.

****

That song and dance shit had lasted about two hours before King and I were on our way to spend some well-deserved and much-needed quality time together alone. It was now two in the morning, but the lust boiling inside of me was giving me the energy that had me ready to fuck my King all night.

King had rented us the most lavish suite in Trump Tower to top off our evening. I would have much rather been at our home, with him in our bed and our daughter a few feet away in her room. But King had been waiting three years for this, and I dared not take this moment away from him. Yet, it was all so overwhelming. This entire day had been so mind-boggling. I hadn't been able to wrap my head around the pampering, the designer clothes, the party, the bottles... and now this. I had been thrust from a small concrete cell to the lap of luxury, but I was too damn horny to focus or enjoy any of it.

"Mmm humph," he moaned as he kissed me on the elevator ride up to our suite. Then he reached down, and his hand disappeared underneath my dress. Just the anticipation of his touch after so long was making me so fucking weak that I damn near lost my balance when his fingers found my hot, pulsating core. "I *cannot* wait to get in this pussy."

The man was only touching me with his fingers, but I was shaking and moaning as if his dick was already inside me. In embarrassment, I turned my head. Now with access to my neck, he buried his face in it as he played with my pussy that was dripping wet around his fingertips. Facing the mirror that lined the elevator, I looked into it and didn't recognize the chick that was looking back at me. Gone were the jumpsuit, the ponytail, and bare face. Suddenly, I was Kennedy again, and my King was right there, just as he'd promised me every day that I was in that hellhole.

The elevator door's opening interrupted our foreplay. His hand reluctantly left the undercarriage of my dress. He took my hand and led me down a short hallway. My heels sunk into carpet that felt as soft as air. No matter what I was once familiar with three years ago, everything was now so new to me. It was like I was smelling, tasting and touching everything for the first time – including *King*.

Seconds after we entered our suite, and he closed the door, we were all over one another. I didn't know what I wanted first. I couldn't decide if I should taste him, or give him a taste of me, or let him thrust that dick inside of me without any foreplay at all. But I didn't have to choose. After laying me across the king-size bed, my man pushed my dress above my waist and dove in face first.

I don't know what felt better; his tongue wrapped around my clit, or the softness of the sheets that I was laying on, or the comfort of the mattress that they encased. All sensations were causing me to fall deeper and deeper into ecstasy... so damn deep that I feared I would burst into my first orgasm in years before the moment that he actually put his dick in me.

"Damn, I missed this pussy," he spoke into my wetness as he sucked my clit, causing my head to rush. I couldn't even form words to go along with my moans and whimpers. I was so full of emotions that I couldn't respond to the spectacular head that he was giving me.

But soon I was embarrassingly cumming into his mouth. I didn't even have to tell him that I was cumming. He could feel it as my body tensed, and my thighs locked. I wanted to tell him how fucking good it felt, but the damn orgasm had hugged my vocal cords and only allowed me to moan and whimper like a damn fool.

Before I could even finish cumming and before my head could stop spinning, he had snatched his shirt off and was hovering above me. Even in the dimly lit room, I could see his dark-chocolate colored skin kissed with tattoos. I ran my hand over his chest, remembering how he once felt and literally thanked God that I was able to touch this man again. But then my hands traveled further, along his erection that was literally throbbing in my grip. He gave me the cutest smirk and, without words, I knew what he was implying. I wanted that dick so bad, but I didn't know if I could handle the ride that he was about to give me. I couldn't count the number of times that King and I had fucked and made love in the two years that we'd spent together before I was sent away. But each time was like some ghetto fairy tale. Birds were chirping on top of the heavy beats of trap music. But now...*this*...the look in his eyes told me that this dick was about to be something that I could not have dreamed about in the time that I had been away.

I was excited but scared. He was so big, and I was so tight from years of being untouched. I hadn't even masturbated because I would never allow anyone else inside of me besides King, not even myself.

JADA

"Damn, I can't believe this pussy still this good after all this time."

That was Dolla; always being funny. He even had to crack a joke or two during sex. We had been fucking for nine years. We had been together for the same amount of time, since we were sixteen, and oddly, nothing had changed.

I giggled as I slapped him on the shoulder. "Shut the fuck up, boy."

He continued to stroke his thick pole slowly in and out of me as he floated above me, resting on his elbows with his eyes looking deeply into mine. "I'm say... s-saying, though... *shit*...I expected this motherfucker not to keep doing this shit to me."

I grinned and began to move my hips in small circles, fucking him back. "Do what to you, baby?"

"*Shit*," he moaned, as his signature hazel eyes rolled to the back of his head.

"Huh?" I asked in a seductively threatening swoon, as the circles of my hips became slower, and I tightened my pussy muscles. "What does this pussy do to you?"

"Shut up, baby."

"Why? Am I making you cum?"

Then Dolla rested on his elbow as he took his other hand and put it over my mouth. With my raunchy words now muffled, his penetration gained a quick tempo that went deep into my pussy and didn't come out until he was spilling his juices.

"Aaaargh!"

Shit, it was crazy to him, but it was also crazy to me that after nine years, feeling him cum gave me just as much satisfaction as my own orgasm.

Before he could fall asleep on top of me, he left the bed and walked into the bathroom of our master bedroom. When he flicked on the light, I could see his rich, brown skin glistening with the moisture of our sex as he dampened a washcloth with soap and water. As he cleaned his manhood, I admired that my man looked the same as the day that I had met him on the first day of school, sophomore year, in Mr. Finley's algebra class. He had the exact same heartbreaker face, with heavy-lidded, bedroom eyes and the slim-fit body of the point guard that he was at the time. Only now, at twenty-five, he was a more mature version of that boy that had asked me to be his girlfriend on a note two weeks later.

We had been rocking together ever since.

"Man, that party was off the chain." His smile was wide while he relived it in his mind as he walked back into the bedroom now holding a new towel. He climbed into bed and began to wipe down my still pulsating pussy. "My nigga, King, was *sooo* happy to see Kennedy. He couldn't stop smiling. I ain't seen that nigga so happy since she went in."

"I don't think any of us have been as happy as we were tonight. We all missed her."

Dolla nodded in agreement as he finished, folded the towel and put it on the nightstand. When he laid down, we instantly spooned with one another.

"That shit was crazy... when she got locked up, man. King ain't been the same since. And even though she's home, I still don't think he'll be the same. The guilt is still there."

I sighed, saying, "I think it's still there in all of us. But now at least she's home."

Another smile crept across my face as the words left my lips, surrounded by shallow breathing, which was an aftershock of me and Dolla's drunk, after-the-club sex. I noticed that after three years, my smile was finally genuine because we were no longer missing a family member. With Kennedy back, all of our smiles were different. Our squad was now whole again. Things felt right, like they did back then before all of this shit went down.

June 2010

five years ago

CHAPTER THREE

KENNEDY

In June of 2010, I had graduated from Thornridge High School. I had also just recently turned eighteen, which was something I had celebrated much more than graduating. Turning eighteen marked my freedom from my father. Don't get me wrong. He wasn't some weird, child molesting, drunk asshole. He was actually quite the opposite. He was a good father and loving, but, gawd damn, if he wasn't smothering and overprotective.

My mother had lost custody of me when I was five years old. She and my father had actually gotten married four years before my birth. While my mother was pregnant with me, she left him because he had found another love interest. It wasn't another woman. It was education and the desire to live life outside of the projects. My mother didn't understand that. She had grown up around hood niggas and gangstas. A man selling dope turned her on way more than a man in a library studying, so she left him for a nigga that everyone in the hood assumed was my father, Big Chino. It was rumored that my mother had been cheating on my dad with Big Chino for a minute, and everyone assumed that I was Big Chino's child. However, I came out the spitting image of my dad.

It took five years for my father to graduate from Chicago State with his Bachelor's and get a job. Then he fought for full custody of me because he thought the dangerous environments that my mother and Big Chino had me in weren't ideal for his one and only, precious daughter. He won that fight and, for the next thirteen years, I was in ballet classes, honors classes, cheerleading and every other extra-curricular activity known to man. Although it was usually a nanny who was watching me, my father ruled with an iron fist from whatever night class he was taking as he earned his master's and doctorate degrees. Since I wasn't eighteen by my prom, he'd even insisted on escorting and chaperoning me and my date to the dance in his vintage, 1936 Mercedes.

Now I had graduated from Thornridge, but I'd never been on a date or even on the phone with a boy, as far as my father knew, and I had a 3.8 GPA. The GPA was real, but the other part was false. I had managed to sneak and have a boyfriend for the past year. He wasn't the corny seventeen-year-old that I'd taken to prom to send my father off either. He was the twenty-year-old that lived around the corner from our brick home in Thornridge.

Like my mother, I had a passion for bad boys that outweighed any common sense that my father had taught me or any intelligence that the books had instilled in me. It was like the more my father told me not to touch them, the more I fantasized about them.

Last summer, before the beginning of my senior year in high school, that fantasy came true. When Reese rode by my father's house in his white Infinity truck, luckily, my old man wasn't home. He hated for me to be home alone once I was too old for a nanny, so he would usually fill my days with summer internships and extracurricular activities. But that day, I had pretended to be sick so that I could stay at home to do what teenagers did during the day in the summer: *nothing*! I had only come outside to feel the summer sun on my skin when Reese drove by me looking like a ghetto knight in shining armor. Laying eyes on him, as he eye-balled me in my Thornridge gym shorts, put me in the mind of any of Wahida Clark's sexy ass thugs that I'd sneak to read behind my father's back in the middle of the night.

Needless to say, when Reese whistled for my attention, I sashayed over to the curb where he was waiting, and we exchanged numbers. I logged him in under the name "Sasha," since my father regularly checked the cell phone that he'd given me. Reese called that night, and we spent hours on the phone. For the past year, I had been sneaking and making up lies to my father in order to spend time with Reese. He had even taken my virginity on the night that I turned eighteen, just two weeks before.

Now, Reese and I would no longer have to sneak. I had been accepted to The University of Chicago. My dream was to attend Spelman. I had fallen in love with the South when my father and I had visited for his family reunions. But he had insisted that I remain under his watchful eye by staying in Chicago and attending the college that he taught at. Plus being a faculty member, any child of his that attended that school received fifty percent off of tuition, which was all my father needed to hear. My grades had earned me a few scholarships, but not enough to cover all of the tuition at Spelman. Though my father was successful, he was cheap and didn't want to *waste* money on the college of my dreams when it was cheaper to go to a school just as great right here in Chicago *and* he could continue to stalk my life.

However, I would be moving to the city closer to the school with my mother. After Big Chino got killed two years ago, she had gotten her life together. Now that she had earned her medical assistant's license, she was working and had finally moved out of the projects. My father felt it was safe for me to stay with her while I attended college. Just to get away from his rules and regulations that much faster, I enrolled in summer classes and was set to move in a week. I was so excited and was walking briskly around the corner to tell Reese that I was finally free. Though I would be staying with my mother, I finally had the freedom to do me. My mother wasn't nearly as strict as my father. During the years as I visited her, she would let me hang out with my cousins on her side, so I knew that I would be able to come and go as I pleased and spend as many nights under Reese that I wanted to.

I was so happy that I was walking blindly. Reese had been so good to me by dealing with my father and his rules. For a year, he had been sneaking and taking me on dates. I had to hide the many gifts that he'd given me, and I couldn't hang out with him and his friends as much as I wanted to. But still, he stayed with me and had even told me that he loved me the night that we first had sex. Because of this, I was ready to be there for him. I wanted to give him my all. Honestly, he was more important to me than the psychology program that I had gotten accepted into. I loved Reese and had dreamed of this day for months, so, needless to say, I nearly skipped my happy ass around that corner toward his townhouse.

Although only twenty, Reese was paid. Like the hustlers I read about, he was one of the more successful local drug dealers. He wasn't one of those dirty niggas that stood on the corner because we lived in too nice of a neighborhood for the Thornridge Police Department to allow that. Reese served coke to these white boys, college kids, and white-collar businessmen. Therefore, he stayed in a luxury townhome in our lavish neighborhood.

I even had a key, and I used it as I hurried into the house, full of excitement and totally ignorant of how unusually quiet it was. Normally, Reese's place would be full of weed smoke and his boys, and usually music would be blasting from the surround sound system, but not this particular afternoon. As I tip-toed through the lower level, I started to second guess coming over unannounced.

Let me check upstairs before I go, I thought to myself. I was so young and dumb then because something should have told me to get the fuck out of there. I was too full of the joy of getting away from my father that I did not realize that I was about to learn the very lessons that he had been trying to teach me. This was what he had told me when he caught me those two times talking to boys when he had forbidden me from doing so; I was about to learn the hard way.

I didn't knock on Reese's bedroom door before opening it. I barged right on in and right smack dab in the middle of his fuck session. He had her bent over on the very blanket that I loved because it felt so good to be wrapped up in it on winter nights when I would sneak over when ditching band practice. Her face was in the bed, his hand was on her neck, and her ass was in the air. I could literally hear how wet she was as the sound of him going in and out of her reminded me of macaroni and cheese. He was so into it. When I saw that he wasn't wearing a condom, I got nauseous, but when I recognized the tattoo of the musical note on her right shoulder blade, I lost it.

"Nikki?" I was too busy flying toward the bed to see their reaction. Before I knew it, I was attempting to climb into the bed with them as she scrambled to cover herself with the sheets. I wanted to rip out every Saga Remy track that I had helped her glue into her hair a few weeks ago. "You fucking bitch!" I was trying my best to dig my nails into those fucking brown eyes, but Reese wouldn't let me get to *her*, my best friend, my ride or die bitch. The chick that had spent the night with me so many times because my father didn't want me spending the night out at anyone else's house. She was the girl who had told me that it was going to be okay when I cried my eyes out because I was so tired of my father's rules. And she was the same bitch that listened when I told her about Reese taking my virginity just two weeks ago.

"Let me go, Reese!" I couldn't understand why he was protecting this bitch. I also couldn't understand why she was sitting calmly in that bed as if she was supposed to fucking be there!

"Chill, Kennedy."

Kennedy. Not *Ken*, the nickname everyone called me, or *baby*, the pet name he always called me, but *Kennedy*, my whole gawd damn government name. The nigga had said every syllable. I looked him in his eyes with disgust, hurt, and disappointment, ready to fire every fucked up word in my head at him.

But then she said, "Just tell her, baby."

32

You ever felt so fucking sick that you just wanted to die? You ever had a nigga or bitch hurt you so fucking bad that you literally felt your heart aching? My daddy had taught me a lot of shit, but he had never told me that heartbreak literally feels like your heart is breaking!

I looked at them not even attempting to hide my confusion. "Baby?"

Nikki huffed at my ignorance, but Reese responded. "Kennedy, me and Nik–"

At least there was some *very* small, minuscule amount of compassion somewhere in his heart for me because he couldn't even say it... so *she* did. "We're fucking, Ken. We've been fucking for the last six months. That's *my* man. He doesn't want you."

I was too hurt to react to the fucked up, sarcastic look on her face. I didn't know who had hurt me more, the nigga that I loved or my best friend for the last four years that I also loved. At that moment, I decided that it was Nikki who had done the most damage. It was most definitely that bitch.

Without another word, I leaped over the bed. As I said, my father had me in a lot of extracurricular activities. During high school, my hips and ass had spread. My once athletic body had fallen victim to the birth control that my father had put me on– yes, though he refused to even let me date–and I was now no longer the teenager with a tight, petite body. I had grown woman curves, but I still jumped on that fucking bed like a track star and tried to kill that bitch.

I could feel Reese over me. "Stop, Kennedy! Chill, man." He was so forceful with me, but, at the time, I didn't even realize it. I also didn't realize that my once feisty friend wasn't fighting me back. She just left the bed and stood far away while Reese held me back.

Like I said before, Nikki was my best friend. I had seen her whoop a bitch a few times, so it puzzled the fuck out of me why she was running away from these hands.

"Stop," Reese insisted again, now with gritted teeth. Then with a hint of sympathy in his voice, he told me, "I'm not going to let you hit her." He paused and grimaced before saying with reluctance, "She's pregnant."

All fight left my body. I stopped struggling as he lay over me on the bed. I looked up at him feeling as if I was going to die. "You said you loved me, Reese. You took my virginity."

And his only reply to taking my precious jewel with maliciousness was a simple ass, emotionless, "I'm sorry."

Still hovering over me, blocking me from Nikki, he stared into my eyes. An awkward silence filled the room for so long that Nikki cleared her throat. As if he remembered that she was there, he told me, "You have to leave."

I was too defeated to fight, so when he stood up to give me room to leave, I left the bed without a further struggle. I turned to leave, now noticing the small belly protruding between Nikki's bra and bare bottom. I then recalled the morning she'd thrown up after she had spent the night and the way she showed disinterest when I frantically called her after Reese and I had had sex for the first time. I was defeated, not only because of how they had tricked me, but because they had proven my father right. I was too hurt to fight anymore, so I just walked out... right after I snatched the lamp from the table that I was passing and hurled it at them both. I wasn't aiming at either one of them in particular, and I didn't give a fuck who I'd hit, but I was sure it was Nikki once I heard her yelp out in pain. My own tears finally began to flow, and unbearable hurt caused me to take flight out of that beautiful ass house.

KING

My wedding day was June 11, 2010. I was the happiest nigga in the world that day. My wife, Tiana Nicole, soon-to-be, Carter, was a hood nigga's dream come true. At twenty-four, a woman had finally been able to sweep me off of my feet. Real talk, she had been on my bumper since we had a math class together freshman year in high school, the last year that I was ever even in school. After I dropped out and decided to study my hustle full-time instead, she still kept up with a nigga; seeing how I was doin', coming by the block to hang out, and all that. But truth be told, for three years I looked shorty over. Don't get me wrong. She was cute with a bad ass body and a pretty smile, but I was young, dumb and full of cum back then. I went through countless bitches, fucking and enjoying the money that I had coming in. But few of those chicks caught my interest. Then the ones that did were much more into my money and how much of it I was giving them to see the potential in the life that I was trying to offer their trifling asses. But Tiana had a nigga's back the entire time. So finally, once I decided to be a real man and wife a bad bitch, I grabbed T-Baby. That was in 2003, and ever since, for the last seven years, she had been the ideal rider. And truth be told, I had been the typical nigga. I was cheating, lying, and putting my baby through hell. No matter how much I loved her, I was young. I didn't appreciate what I had at home, and I found myself in random pussy every now and then. I did love her, though, and, last year, when I saw that she was at her wits end, I put a ring on it.

Now, I was standing in a meeting room at Faith Tabernacle, one of the biggest churches in the Chi, putting the finishing touches on my Armani suit so that I could stand at the altar and watch my beautiful bride walk down the aisle.

"King!" Siren's voice was coupled with a hard round of knocks that sounded serious. "King!"

"What? Come in! Damn!" I stayed focused on straightening out my bowtie in the full-length mirror as Siren barged in. Through the mirror, I admired how well she had cleaned up for the occasion. Her blue...teal...whatever the hell...fitted bridesmaids dress had her curves popping.

Tiana was tight with Siren, as well as my right hand's girl, Jada. Jada and Dolla had been together since high school. Since Dolla was my right-hand man and Jada was her best friend, Siren was deeply affiliated with my squad. Therefore, Tiana was constantly around Jada and Siren, thought they were friends, so made them bridesmaids in the wedding as well.

"I need to talk to you, King,"

I discreetly huffed as I perfected the design that my locks were styled in. "Now is not a good time, Siren."

She sucked her teeth. "Seriously!"

"Now is not–"

"Nigga!" She had grabbed me by my elbow and started dragging me out of the room.

"What the fuck is you doin'?!"

"Sshh! C'mon!"

She looked serious as shit, so I shut up and followed her. The rest of the wedding party was supposed to be lined up in the lobby, ready to march in. Dolla and Meech, my best men, were already posted at the altar. That's why I couldn't understand what the fucking emergency was. But with Siren, I never knew, so I was cautious than a motherfucka as she peeked around corners while dragging me through the second level of the church.

For years, Siren had been pulling one trick or another out of her ass to get my attention. I couldn't blame her. I had been fucking her off and on since we were shorties. She was one of the bitches that I ran through on a late night when I was drunk and had a hard dick. She was different than the rest, though. We had actually become close friends over the years, and since being introduced to my crew, she had run a lot of drugs for me, holding me, Meech, and Dolla down. She was the classic ride or die bitch, but in the back of my mind, I always felt like it wasn't genuine. It was obvious that she liked Jada's life, wanted the same, and I was the first name on her list. Beyond that, I just never had feelings for shorty like that. She knew it, but she continued to throw the pussy at me every now and then. Even after I wifed Tiana down, she had the pussy open on my gullible, weak nights.

In the last year, she was the only chick that I had even cheated on Tiana with. But the closer the wedding day approached, Siren became clingy and jealous, trying to find every reason why I shouldn't marry Tiana. She always said I shouldn't trust her and that she was cheating on me, but of course *she* would say that. So six months ago, I had to cut off her dick supply.

"What the fuck is goin' on, Siren?"

She put her hand over my mouth as we approached a door. Then she whispered, "Listen to this shit."

Siren was a trip, but besides being infatuated with me, I could trust her with my life and my business. So I stood quietly at the door and listened.

"I'm marrying him because you didn't wanna fucking be with me," I could hear Tiana saying. "*Now* you wanna be with me? The day of my fucking wedding? *Now* you love me, Money?"

Money. My heart dropped to my feet. I knew Money. He was a hustler on the South Side too. He was getting money, hence the nickname, but not like the money that I was getting and the potential that I had to get even more. We knew each other from being in the same business and had even broken bread and popped bottles together a few times. But we didn't have any beef...until now.

Siren watched me with a smirk that said, "I told you so!" But I ignored that shit and kept listening.

"I gave you every opportunity to be with me." I could literally hear the tears as Tiana tried to cry quietly. It was obvious that she was on the phone with this nigga. "You wanted to fuck those other hoes. You wouldn't choose me, so I chose him."

Man, I ain't listening to no more of this shit, I thought as I turned on my heels.

"Where are you going?" Siren whispered harshly, running after me as I stormed away from the door. "You ain't gonna say nothing to this bitch? You still gonna marry her?"

I just kept walking, trying to tune her ass out and think fast. Hell nah, I wasn't marrying her ass. But if I had killed Tiana in that church, I would be in jail and going straight to hell, so I had to get the fuck up out of there.

When I stormed by the bridal party, they all looked at me like I was crazy as I barged through the doors of the sanctuary. As soon as Dolla and Meech saw my face, they knew that something was wrong. My boys left the altar and jogged down the aisle toward me as the entire congregation looked on in curiosity and confusion. Even Jada was on my heels, leaving the bridesmaids line the moment that she realized something was wrong.

"What's wrong?" Meech asked me as he followed me out of the congregation.

I spit over my shoulder, "We out this bitch."

"What?" Dolla asked with a slight chuckle. "Bruh, what's goin' on? What happened?"

"That bitch is fucking with Money," I said just as Siren appeared.

That was all that needed to be said. They all followed me out of the church without another question, while the bridal party was looking on with eyes full of questions.

But as soon as the sun hit my face, something told me that I couldn't go out like that. I turned and looked at Jada and Siren. "Go handle that bitch for me."

Jada reluctantly followed orders out of loyalty, but Siren was more than fucking happy to do so. They weren't gonna kill her like I wanted them to do in my heart, but they definitely were about to beat the brakes off of that bitch.

June 2010

Chapter Four

Kennedy

The knock on my bedroom door sounded like roaring, deafening thunder. My head felt like it had been hit by a Mack Truck. My heart was so heavy, and I had no strength. My heart literally hurt...like I felt the damn pain in my chest cavity, and it increased every time the image of Reese on top of my best friend played in my mind. The ache increased every time I looked at the phone and saw no missed call or text message from either one of them apologizing or trying to fix it. I had been crying for three days straight, and the strain on my heart had traveled to my brain, causing me to wince every time my father knocked heavily on the thin, wooden door.

"Kennedy! Kennedy, get up."

"Urggh," I groaned, pulling the covers over my head.

"Kennedy, open this door! It's late. Stop laying around like a bum."

Shit like that made me despise my loving father. I was eighteen, so what was wrong with me laying around until noon on a summer day? Moreover, he was my father, and my heart was crushed. Yet, I couldn't even talk to him about it. I couldn't crawl onto his lap, lay my head on his shoulder, and get those encouraging, loving words like, "It's going to be okay, baby girl. Your knight in shining armor will come one day." No, I couldn't do that without being punished with some two-hour-long lecture about how I shouldn't have been talking to boys anyway. He treated me like I was twelve years old or some shit.

After another round of knocks that were now so hard that they shook the door, I threw the covers back and dragged myself toward the door, still wearing the gown that I had put on three days ago after leaving Reese's house and hiding in my bed as I cried myself to sleep. I opened it without even acknowledging my father, but I noticed how he strolled in wearing a navy, slim fit suit that hugged his tall, slender frame perfectly. Leave it to my father to be suited and booted on a Saturday before noon. Knowing him, he was going to the office on his day off to do research.

I simply went to my dresser to gather toiletries for my shower while trying to hide the hurtful tears in my eyes.

"Kennedy, I don't know what's gotten into you, but you need to get yourself together and stop being such a... *bum*." The last word came out forced as if it hurt his throat to use such a simple word.

That hurt. If anything, I had worked myself like a fucking slave through high school, getting good grades, going to after school programs, and studying until midnight. My father might not have known about the secrets that I'd kept about Reese, but if anything, he knew that I was far from a bum.

"A bum? Daddy, what's bummie about chillin' during the summer?" I was surprised at my own aggressiveness. I wasn't being rude, but I had always been a "yes, sir" type of child. I hated how he treated me, but I had always respected him.

He sensed the disrespect too. I could see the disapproval all over his face through the mirror as I shifted through shower gels. He was standing behind me with his arms folded, threateningly and wearing a scowl. "*Chillin'*?" he repeated with a voice laced with disgust. "Don't use that language in this house."

I had to literally put an imaginary chokehold on my chuckle. My father was so transparent. He only hated everything ghetto because it reminded him too much of the man who'd stolen his wife from him. Instead of chuckling, I sighed inwardly as he continued.

"I can't have this. You've graduated from high school, but that doesn't mean that the work stops. It's only begun."

"I know that, Dad. That's why I'm starting summer school in a few weeks."

"And until then you could be doing some research, study...anything to qualify you for more scholarships next year. Have you done anything to better yourself? No. You've been laying around for days crying over a boy like some...some... *hoodrat*!"

I spun around on the balls of my feet with even more hurt in my heart. "Hoodrat?" came out of my throat coated in tears as they welled in my eyes.

But he ignored my hurt. "I overheard your conversation with Jada last night, and I cannot *believe* that you would defy me by having some relationship with some ghetto thug!"

Obviously, he hadn't heard everything about me and Reese, because if he had known that I was no longer a virgin, he would've been tearing this motherfucking room up instead of looking at me like I was filth.

"So I'm a hoodrat because I had a boyfriend? I'm eighteen. Most girls my age have boyfriends. So, they're all hood rats?"

His lips pressed together tightly as he took a step towards me. "Girl, don't you question me!"

Looking back, I know that my anger wasn't really toward him. Yes, he irritated me. That was nothing new. I was suddenly standing up to him because I had wanted to have this battle with Reese. "I'm just trying to understand, Daddy. I have a 3.8 GPA. I do everything you say. I have carpel tunnel in my wrists from all of the papers that I've stayed up all night typing. I have calluses on the bottom of my feet from constant dance practices and cheerleading! I went hard no matter how tired I was."

"And that's what you *should* have done! I don't feel sorry about any of that. I do not feel sorry for making sure that you turned out right. You should be more grateful that I was a good enough father not to allow you to end up like your mother."

His last words made me wince in pain. I was so sick of the men in my life, who were supposed to love me, hurting me on purpose.

"You want to end up barely making it, the uneducated widow of a gawd damn thug that left no benefits after his death because he'd never had a real job to earn any Social Security? Is that what you want? *Huh?!*"

There was no use. Fighting with my dad was plain useless. We were arguing with each other but we were hurting over someone else. He was still hurting over my mother, and I was simmering in heartbreak over Reese.

So I just simply told him, "No, sir," as I collected my toiletries. "May I be excused to the bathroom?"

I was too tired to fight or to say another word. So when he said, "Go," with a dismissive wave of the hand, I just went, prepared to fill my day with hard work, just like he wanted me to...*packing*!

SIREN

"What up, Siren?"

King didn't even bother lifting his head from the computer as I walked into his home office. A glass of Remy sat on the desk. I could imagine that he was trying to drink away the urge to find Money, shoot him, and throw his bowlegged, big head ass in Lake Michigan.

Since the wedding day, I kept asking him why he had let Money live. His answer was that he refused to confront another man about a broad. It was a man code that he refused to violate, though he wanted to break Money's fucking neck. Tiana had gotten hers, though. Jada and I had emerged from the church about five minutes after going in. We'd beaten the shit out of Tiana while she was still in the pretty ass wedding gown. She was still on the phone with Money when we barged into the room. She was not even aware that King had walked out on her ass.

A broken jaw later, she knew, though. She had gotten a clear message that she would never be Mrs. Damion Carter.

I rounded the wooden desk with a backpack on my back. As I stood in front of him, I took it from my shoulders, dropped down to the floor, and opened it.

"You counted it while you were there, right?" he asked me, still staring at the computer.

"Yeah, but you know me. I gotta count twice."

That was me; I was always doing extra to show King that I was fit to be sleeping next to him in his kingdom.

I had done a drop for the squad that evening. In the bag should have been ninety-five thousand dollars, which is how much they charged Big C, this guy out west, for six bricks. If King's love life was going down the drain, the money was definitely overflowing from his business. It was the second run that I had made that week.

"What's good with you?"

I looked at King curiously as he waited for an answer. He should have understood my surprise. For a long time, he had been distant from me because he was trying to be loyal to a bitch that didn't even deserve it.

I tried to play it cool. "I'm good. Been chasing after Elijah's hyper ass all day."

King chuckled. "Yeah, he *is* hyper. You need to get that nigga on Ritalin or something."

I had to laugh too. "Whatever. Leave my son alone." Then, as I pulled the bundles of cash wrapped in rubber bands from the Coach book bag, I asked, "How are you?" while unraveling a few and starting to count.

"I'm good," he quickly told me, speaking into the Remy as he took a sip.

"You're lying."

He chuckled, saying, "I'm good, yo'," as he tried to act like he was into the work on the computer, which I could clearly see was really his Facebook timeline. He was supposed to be going over the books that his accountant had sent him for his restaurant, but he looked like he couldn't focus for shit.

When he heard me sigh, he looked down at me and noticed how genuinely concerned I looked. Besides being his booty call, I had been a friend for years. I knew him, so he knew that I knew he was lying and that I wanted the truth.

"A'ight," he admitted with a smile. "I'm irritated as fuck."

"You should be."

"I never expected that shit. You tried to tell me. I'm sorry for not listening."

That apology spoke more to me than just those two simple words. For a moment, I was wide-eyed and temporarily speechless. Then I exhaled as my eyes changed from concerned to loving. As always, the moment that King showed one ounce of emotion toward me, I took it and ran with it. He had only apologized, but the fact that he had even cared that much was the small crack in a partially opened door that I needed.

I sat the cash I held in my hands on the floor and literally crawled to him, my ass visible in its heart shape as my back stayed arched during my journey toward him. I knew he saw in my eyes what I wanted, and, as he took another sip of Remy, I knew what he needed to temporarily make his irritations go away.

"I just wanted you to know that she didn't deserve you." My voice was now a sweet whisper. I had gone from dropping off dope and counting money to being a seductress. "You thought I was hating, when really I was just being loyal, baby. I knew she wasn't good for you."

I didn't even ask his permission as I started to unbuckle his belt. Like I said, I was his friend. I knew him, so I knew that even though he had been telling me no for so long, at the moment, he was weak and needed what I had been throwing at him so desperately for the last six months. "You deserve so much better than a bitch like that." I was literally crooning girlishly as I gently pulled his dick out of his G-Star jeans. I said, "You're a boss," just as I slid his dick through my full lips and wet mouth and started to suck. "And you deserve a boss bitch," I spoke through slurps. "Somebody who's going to be loyal." Slurp...gag...slurp...moan... "Somebody who's going to be down." I slurped, gagged, and moaned some more. "You're fucking *King Carter*. You deserve a queen."

Behind those words was my desperation to be his queen, and as usual, if I thought pussy was going to slide me into that queendom, then he let me use it to convince him.

I knew that he hadn't fucked in two weeks because Tiana had this crazy idea that they should be abstinent for a while to make their honeymoon that much more special. Bitch was probably fucking Money the whole time.

I took King's hand and put it on my ponytail. Taking the hint, he grabbed it and started to deliberately but slowly fuck my mouth.

"Mmm…" The roughness turned me on, and I took his long length like a champ…like Superhead herself.

"Grrr…" The absence of pussy and head for so long and the tightness of my throat had caused a raspy, sexy moan to barrel out of his throat as he continued to stroke my tonsils.

I continued to gag, and saliva spilled all over his steel, hard dick, making it wet and ready to get in that pussy.

"Come here. Come sit on it."

I was more than happy to oblige. I was sure that he had never seen a woman get out of tight shorts so fast in his life. I would have ripped them off if I could have.

As soon as I straddled him and lowered myself onto his dick, I started to moan like this was the best dick of my life. "Mmm! I missed this big dick."

My arms rested behind his head on the back of the chair. We were face to face, and mouth to mouth, but when I came in for a kiss, he turned his head, yet grabbed my ass and smacked it just like I liked it.

"Yes," I breathed. "Fuck yes."

The pussy that I was giving him was unhurried. It was slow and too sensual for him, and I knew it. It was making love, but we weren't about that, so he held on tight to my waist and started giving me mean strokes that slaughtered the pussy.

"Oooh, yes, King! Yes!" I squealed. "Fuck me!"

Despite the fact that it was plainly obvious that he was going out of the way to fuck me and not make love to me, I couldn't help but respond submissively to the dick.

"You want this dick?"

"Yes!"

"Tell me how much."

"I want it," I insisted as I stood on my tiptoes and started to fuck him back. "Give me this dick, King."

That's what he wanted; raunchy, slutty, and dirty sex, and not slow and loving like I wanted. But I guessed he felt like it wasn't what I deserved.

July 2010

Chapter Five

Kennedy

Two weeks after catching Nikki and Reese, I moved out of my father's house. I had been waiting on the day for so long. Throughout the years, every time that I imagined the day that I moved out, I knew that I would be ecstatic, but I never knew that I would be so happy to get away from my father *and* Reese.

Eventually, Reese called. I felt better that he actually cared enough to reach out, but it didn't make the hurt go away because, when he called, and never stopped calling, my heart was still broken. For two weeks, Reese had been trying to explain. But how could he explain that shit? He had been fucking my girl for God knows how long! Then the snake bastard took my virginity as a parting gift. Fuck his explanations! So I ignored every call. For once, I was happy that my father was so damn overprotective because if he wasn't, Reese probably would have showed up at my house.

And you know what? Not one of those voicemails said that he was sorry, that he loved me, or that it was a mistake. They were just attempted explanations that I deleted before completely listening to because they just sounded like some bullshit excuse for why he fucked my girl.

But you know who never called? Nikki! But fuck that bitch and fuck him. I was so happy to be away from them and out of that neighborhood. It felt like I was starting all over, but I can't lie; that shit had hurt like a bitch, and that hurt was written all over my face.

"Urgh, Kennedy, would you fix your face? You can't go up in here lookin' like that." That was my older cousin, Jada.

I was riding in the backseat of her Benz while her best friend, Siren, rode gunshot. Jada was my first cousin on my mother's side. Her father, Uncle Ryan, and my mother were fraternal twins, so she and I looked a lot alike. Siren and Jada had met in grammar school and had been best friends ever since. The few times when my father had allowed me to visit my mother, I always hung out with them, so I had become pretty cool with Siren too. Though they were four years older than me, they always let me hang out on the block with them. Jada's boyfriend was some hood nigga, Dolla, who sold dope out south. So Jada was always under him in one of the trap houses or on the block with one of his partners,

Meech. King was the other part of their crew, but I was told that he was older than us all. He was really the money behind their whole organization, so he was rarely on the block putting his hands on the work. Like I said before; unfortunately, I was like my mother. I loved the hood and the lifestyle that came along with it. It was a fantasy that was only magnified by the books that I read, so I was mesmerized every time I hung out with them.

Anyway, of course, Jada and Siren were the first people that I called when I was all moved in.

"I'm sorry," I told Jada with a sigh.

"You need a drank," Siren said with a giggle.

"Girl, I'm only eighteen. I can't drink. My father would kill me. Oh, but wait! Daddy ain't here!"

Jada and Siren started cracking up, and, for the first time that day, I finally cracked a smile.

As we turned onto a side street and Jada began to slow down, she told me, "You can drink, but I ain't lettin' you get drunk. Your daddy ain't here, but I'm not trying to hear Auntie's mouth. You're on a one drink limit."

"Cool with me." Shit, I had never had more than one really diluted drink anyway, and that was when I was sneaking whiskey out of my father's stash, so I was cool with that.

As we parked in front of an apartment building, I noticed all of these guys standing outside. I could see them discreetly selling baggies to cluckers that walked by. They would also try to holla at chicks that walked by in itty bitty shorts and skirts. It was the end of June and warm as hell...the best time to live in the Chi. I even had on a pair of jean dukes. My thick thighs and hips fell out of the backseat as I climbed out of the car and waited on Siren and Jada. I could hear the guys making lewd remarks about my ass as I stood with my back to them, but I could already tell that they were lil' dirty boys that stood outside all day selling werk. Sure, they were making money, but I had already dated a nigga that was above their level. I couldn't take that many steps back. Besides that, Reese had me rethinking my hood nigga fetish anyway. Along with a man with money and hood fame, came bitches...lots of 'em. I was trying to recover from what Reese had done to me, so I was to be damned if I put myself in another situation like that.

Daddy was so right, I thought as I followed Jada and Siren into the building. I ignored the way the guys stared at me and even tried to get my attention by gently grabbing my elbow. *I need a gentleman. These niggas ain't shit.*

The attention didn't stop when we walked into apartment 3B. As soon as we walked into the smoke-filled apartment, it was like all conversation stopped. I recognized a few of the homies, but they were looking at me like they had never seen me before. I knew that I had started to wear my hair down and a little make-up, and that my hips had spread, but *damn*! They were staring so hard that I was starting to feel insecure, like I should put some clothes on.

"Damn, Kennedy, all eyes on you," Siren muttered as we walked through the living room. I hid how uncomfortable I was and just smiled as she sucked her teeth and said, "Hey everybody! Damn!"

"Aye, Siren," a guy greeted from the couch. "What up tho?"

"Nothing much. Just watching y'all drool over my girl. Her name is Kennedy, by the way. Stop being rude and speak."

I blushed and waved, but kept walking, following Jada into the kitchen. I was on her heels. As soon as we entered the kitchen, I peeped a guy sitting in the corner at the table with his head down clutching a bottle of Jameson. Seconds after Jada spoke to Meech and Dolla, who were also sitting at the table, the dude looked up. He was the finest motherfucka alive, I swear!

I hated a pretty nigga, and he was far from that. He was rough all over with the prettiest eyes I'd ever seen among so many tattoos. His dreads were pulled into a ponytail. And that poor chair; it was so small compared to how big he was. I feared it would break.

He quickly spoke to Jada and Siren, who had skipped into the kitchen in front of me. "What up, y'all?" Then, he was about to put his head right back down until he caught me staring.

Fuck! I quickly lowered my eyes and started fidgeting with my tube top nervously.

"You straight, King?" I heard Siren ask, and then I automatically looked back up and into his eyes, which were still trying to discreetly look at me.

King... So that's him, I silently concluded.

"Yeah, I'm good," he told Siren. Then he and Meech gave each other a look that only they understood.

Then Meech smirked before saying, "What's up, Kennedy? What you doin' out this way?"

King looked back and forth between me and Meech. He was surprised that Meech was actually familiar with me.

"She's going to the University of Chicago. She starts next week," Jada answered proudly. She was always so proud of me and bragged about how smart I was. "My cousin is going to *coooollege,*" she teased as she lightly pushed me with her hip.

Again, I just blushed as I couldn't help but notice King really looking at me now because all eyes in the kitchen were on me.

"Straight? That's what's up," Meech told me. "What are you gonna major in?"

"Psychology."

"What you gon' do with that?"

"I want to be a child and adolescent psychologist."

"*What?*" Meech asked as he looked at me suspiciously. "And you from Chicago?"

Siren sucked her teeth. "What the hell is that supposed to mean?"

"*Shiiiid,*" Meech replied. "It ain't a lot of pretty girls that are smart too out here in these streets–"

"Excuse you!" Siren spit.

"Exactly!" Jada added.

"Are any one of you motherfuckas in school? I'm just saying," Meech laughed.

When Dolla joined in on the snickering, Jada gave him an evil stare, and he shut right the fuck up.

Mind you, while all of this was going on, King was still checking me out. I had started to act like I didn't see him and gave Meech's conversation my undivided attention.

"Anyway, shorty, that's what's up for real," he told me. "I'm proud of you. Don't be in these streets hanging with these motherfuckers and get off track. Matter fact, get the hell out of Chicago altogether."

"I wanted to," I said with a sigh. "I wanted to go to Spelman down in Atlanta."

"So why not go?"

"My daddy wouldn't pay for it because he wants me to stay here. And my mother can't afford to send me so..."

Meech simply nodded his head like he understood.

"Anyway, I'm ready to pour up," Siren interrupted as she stood among the guys at the table. "What you want, Jada?"

"1800. You already know," Jada answered. "What you want, Kennedy?"

I glanced over at the table. "Any whiskey?"

Again, all eyes were on me.

"*Whiskey*?! What the hell?!" Jada squealed.

I shrugged as I answered, "That's what my daddy drinks."

Then King's voice eased through the air like a sultry, R&B classic. "You can come and drink with me, shorty."

Shit, even his voice was sexy. I was hesitant at first, but then Jada gave me a look like "Bitch, you betta get over there," so I made my way while King actually pulled a chair over toward him for me to sit down. As I eased into the seat, he began pouring me a drink into a plastic red cup. All I could think was, *Just one drink, bitch.*

KENNEDY

But did I listen to myself? No! I started throwing 'em back, trying my best to drink my heartache away. Sure, King was fine, but overall, it felt so fucking good to be having a good time without worrying about my daddy. And every time I finished a drink, my heart hurt less and less.

"Shorty, you better slow down."

King and I had finished a fifth of Jameson on our own, and we were on to the next one. We had migrated out of the kitchen and were on the couch in the living room. It was now pretty late, after midnight. So, many of the guys who were hanging out when I arrived were gone. It was just me, the girls, Dolla, Meech, and King. A few block boys were still out serving, so they were coming in and out as we kicked it and listened to music while the TV played a movie that none of us was watching. The girls, Meech, and Dolla were on the other side of the room smoking, but neither me nor King smoked weed.

"I'm good," I told him as I sipped from my cup.

King's right eyebrow rose, questioning my bravery. "You sure?"

"I promise."

"A'ight," he said, shrugging his shoulders. "So finish telling me what happened. Did he tell you why?"

I was so drunk that my mouth was going fifty miles an hour. I had started telling King all about how I'd caught Reese and Nikki fucking.

"He kept calling my phone for days trying to explain," I slurred.

"What he say?"

When I shrugged, my shoulders felt heavy as hell. *Yep, I'm drunk*, I had to admit to my damn self. But I wasn't sloppy drunk. However, one more drink would've pushed my ass over the edge. I would've embarrassed myself. *This is the last one*, I promised myself.

"I didn't answer and I never listened to his messages."

"So how do you know how he really felt about you?

"Should I care?"

He was about to answer when a shadow came over us. It was Siren.

"Jada is about to ride out with Dolla, Kennedy. Meech already left."

Both King and I looked around curiously. We had been so wrapped up in our conversation that we didn't hear anyone leave over it and the music.

"Jada said you can drive yourself home," Siren continued. Then she handed me the keys as I mentally questioned whether I should be driving Jada's pretty ass Benz or not in my present state.

"But how are *you* gonna get home?" I asked her.

I guess the reluctance was written all over my face because King cut Siren off before she could even answer, telling her, "She can't drive," as he snatched the keys from me.

Siren huffed as she took the keys out of King's hand. "Fine. I'll take her home. How long are you going to be out south?" she asked him.

There was some tension between them that I didn't understand.

"I'll take her home," King told her, staring into her eyes.

I literally saw her swallow hard as she answered, "Okay. You cool with that, Kennedy? You straight?"

"Yeah, I'm good." Whether I really was or not, I didn't know. I was just having fun for once, and I wasn't ready to end my night. Plus, talking to King was cool. He was eight years older than me, so he had been dropping a lot of knowledge on me about Reese that was helping me understand my situation.

"She's good," King reiterated as Siren continued to stand there.

"A'ight," she sighed. It was obvious that she felt some type of way about me being there with King, which I could understand. I was still so young, and she and Jada often looked out for me like a little sister. "I'm out then."

As soon as Siren turned around to leave, King turned to me. "Fuck! It's hot in here," he grunted as he actually started to take off his shirt. As soon as Siren closed the door behind her, he was shirtless.

Shit! Damn, he looked good! Suddenly, I wasn't as drunk as I had been earlier, and I remembered how fine this nigga was. His fucking chest was calling me. I just wanted lay my head on that motherfucka and suck my thumb. Whew!

"Yeah, you should care."

I heard him, but I was too busy staring at the tattoo that covered his entire chest.

"Hello? Did you hear me?"

I snapped out of it. "Huh?" When he smiled bashfully, my pussy got wet.

"I said you should care."

Then I remembered what we were talking about before Siren interrupted us, but I did not want to talk about Reese anymore. Suddenly, I felt stupid as hell for sitting with this fine ass nigga for hours and talking about another nigga.

So stupid, I thought as I snuck glances at his body. His chest was all sweating from the lack of central air. There was one air conditioner in the window, but it was doing nothing really. The sweat on the surface of his skin had him looking like melting chocolate, and I just wanted to lick him up.

The only man that I had had sex with was Reese. Now here I was drunk with any girl's hood nigga dream and didn't know the first thing about seducing him. I would have liked to. My drunk mind wanted him to fuck me until I couldn't remember who Reese was. But he had been a gentleman all night, and I thought he wasn't even interested until he asked, "Did he hurt you?"

And the sincerity and protection in his voice made me melt– literally. I answered honestly, "Yeah. He did."

His stare was so intense as he asked, "What you want me to do about it?"

I gasped inwardly and let my drunk mind speak my sober truth. "Fuck me until I forget."

KING

I had looked deep into her eyes before I asked this next question because I wanted her to feel exactly what I was feeling. "What you want me to do about it?"

She looked like I had kinda taken her breath away as she answered, "Fuck me until I forget."

And that was all a nigga needed to hear. I leaned over and started kissing her neck as I slid my hand under tube top.

Yes! I thought when I felt bare titties and no bra. Shit, shorty was pretty, but she was thick as fuck! Most of my niggas liked them little chicks, but I liked ass, titties, and big legs, and shorty here had it all. It was probably a lil' risky hitting one of Siren's girls, but she had always been good at keeping her mouth shut about us fucking around because her doing otherwise meant that I was cutting her off altogether. She knew I didn't play that shit.

Regardless, my dick was so hard that I didn't give a fuck. I'm not gon' lie. Tiana had fucked a nigga's head up completely. So much so that I hadn't done shit for two weeks, but make money. Before fucking Siren two weeks ago, I hadn't had any pussy for a minute because Tiana wanted us to be abstinent for a while before the wedding so that our honeymoon would be extra special. And after leaving her at the altar, the last thing I was thinking about was another lying ass, opportunist ass bitch and her pussy. So despite her many advances, I hadn't hit Siren again since.

I still had a mind to kill that nigga, Money, but I would have looked like a simple nigga for body bagging another man over some pussy. So I put all of my anger into focusing on my money and flipping bricks faster than my connect could re-up. I was trappin' literally. At first, it had got to the point that I wasn't even coming to the block, but I was so focused on my money that I was now right in the trap with my niggas, watching my money come, which is why I happened to be in the trap that day.

I wasn't even thinking about fucking until I saw this pretty young thang walk into the kitchen earlier. Shorty made my dick wake up after two weeks. Not only was she sluggin', but she was chocolate, just the way I liked them, with a smile that lit up this fucking trap house.

"You got a condom, right?"

I had already laid her down and slid off her shorts. I was kneeling in-between her legs on the couch. Even in my drunk state, as she looked up at me, something told me that it was something different about her that was going to change my life, even though all I wanted was a nut for the night.

"Yeah, I got you," I told her as I reached into the window seal where we kept the rubbers.

Shorty looked like she was contemplating this whole thing, so I hurriedly unbuckled my pants and only slid them down enough to give me room to tear this pussy up. As soon as my dick was revealed, I saw her eyes buck, but when she saw me looking, she looked away.

"You okay?"

She just nodded as I hovered over her, brought my dick to her opening and used it to play with her pussy.

"Mmmmm." When she started to moan, I figured she was cool, so I started sucking her titty to keep her there. Her breath got short as she put her fingers in my dreads and ran them across my scalp. That shit made me want to go straight past go, so I slid right in as my tongue made circles around her nipple.

"Shit!" she said as we both gasped.

I immediately wanted to just pound that pussy out, but I couldn't. I had to take it slow and steady because with each stroke, her pussy was pulling out my nut, and I wasn't ready to cum. "Damn, your pussy is tight."

The only response I got was, "Mmm! Oh, shit!"

I felt the same way, but to keep from sounding like a complete bitch, I just bit my lip and hid my face in her neck. But that shit wasn't working. Her pussy was so tight that I was steadily fighting the urge to cum. "*Damn*, this pussy so fucking tight. How old are you?"

"Huh?" she giggled with deep breaths.

"How old are you?" I asked again, fighting past my lust to look at her curiously.

"I'm eighteen."

"You sure?" I asked, pushing back the urge to tell her how good her pussy was.

Her breath was still choppy as she asked, "Are you going to stop fucking me to check my ID?"

"Hell nah." No matter how old she was, it was too late. This pussy had a nigga turning into a one minute man, and it was so good that I didn't care. She could talk about me to Jada and Siren; I didn't give a fuck. I was about to cum. I sat up, held on to her waist, and got in the pussy so that that we both could enjoy the fuck out of this two minutes.

"Shit! Oh my God!"

"Fuck!" left my mouth unexpectedly. "Shit. Damn, Reina."

There was a slight pause in my stroke as shock hit me. *Did I just call her that? I'm trippin',* I thought to myself as I resumed my stroke like nothing ever happened.

She looked at me like I was crazy, but I just leaned over and sucked her bottom lip as I fought a losing battle with this pussy. I tried to sign my name on that motherfucker just because it had the nerve to be so fucking good.

"Mmm! Yes, King! Oh my God!" The way she moaned was even sexy. That pretty ass young voice sounded like a porno and filled up the trap house. I had never heard bad words sound so sweet. Each time I went in that pussy, she encouraged me with her moans and whimpers. Though it was going to be fast, I knew that I was giving her this dick, drunk or not. At first she was stiff, but after a few more strokes, she started to fuck me back saying, "Yes, give me this dick."

And it was a wrap! I was cumming. A few more deep strokes into that tight space and it was over. "Aaaargh!" I leaned against the back of the couch for support as I held the top of the condom and slid out. We both sat there, paralyzed, staring at each other while we tried to catch our breath.

"Now…," I breathed as I tapped her knee. "… let me see that ID."

SIREN

Hurt was an understatement. King had just completely played me for that little, young ass girl. Kennedy was beautiful. There was no denying that. She was smart too. When she moved in with her mother and started hanging out with us, I expected these hood niggas to drool all over her, but not *King*. She was too young and too innocent for him.

It's like King took every opportunity to choose someone else over me. I thought that was over once I proved that Tiana was disloyal. But tonight he'd done it again. When I was standing there in front of that couch, he knew what I wanted. Ever since we had fucked that night in his office, I had been trying to get some more of that good dick. That night, if I had forgotten how good he felt, how much being with him made me whole, I was reminded. My intent to become Mrs. King Carter was refueled. But once again, he had burst my bubble by dodging me or making excuses why we couldn't hang out. And now he was hanging out with Kennedy, my friend, and I knew... I just knew he was giving her my dick.

Yes, she was beautiful, but I had what she didn't have; his motherfucking back. Even when I saw him staring at her in the kitchen, I never once expected him to actually talk to her. King chose his women carefully, even his booty calls. He was in the game too deep and had way too much money to thoughtlessly put his dick in some random chick. So if he chose a woman, she was special in one way or another. Even I was special because he trusted me. I had his back, and I was loyal.

But what the fuck did he see in Kennedy's young ass over me? If he'd chosen her for the night, she was special to him, and that thought left me nauseous as I drove Jada's car through the city. I had already watched him be with another woman. After fucking him for years and witnessing him wife Tiana, I had post-traumatic stress syndrome. He could only be trying to dick her down for the night, but it scared the shit out of me. The possibility of her being in his life for one hour or a lifetime was making me sick with jealousy just the same.

July 2010

CHAPTER SIX

KENNEDY

I hadn't been fucking for a whole month and I was already doing the walk of shame.

It was two in the morning, so after King and I got dressed and cleaned up in the bathroom, I told him to take me to Jada and Dolla's house. I didn't want my mother to see a nigga dropping me off so late when I had just moved in. Luckily, Jada was awake and texted me back, saying that it was okay for King to bring me there.

We were riding down the Bishop Ford in King's Camaro toward Jada and Dolla's house when I heard him ask over the music, "You want some breakfast?"

"No," I barely said aloud. "I'm okay."

I just wanted to go lay down. I was already hungover from the Jameson and that dick. It was so fucking good, but I was starting to sober up and realize what I had done. I had gone from a virgin to letting Reese fuck me up so much that I was giving nigga's pussy on the first night. And it wasn't even technically the "first night," because tonight wasn't a date, and King hadn't expressed any interest in taking me out before I just gave him some pussy.

He simply said, "A'ight," and turned back up Lil' Wayne's *Tha Carter III*.

For the next ten minutes, we rode in complete silence. I was definitely regretting fucking him. Now that I was sobering up, I recalled everything I had heard Jada and Siren say about King. He was that nigga. He was hood rich. He was a hot commodity, and every chick in the Midwest wanted him. He had turned out most of them. And I had completely slutted myself out to him.

Typical.

I believed that he was starting to regret it too because, as we pulled up in front of Jada's house, all he said was, "A'ight, shorty. I'll holla at you."

But how could he if he hadn't even asked for my number? So even though he was about to get out to open my door for me, I stopped him. "I got it," I said as I swung the door up. "It was nice meeting you."

I got out of that car so fast that I couldn't even hear what he was saying as I closed the door and did a light jog toward Jada's front door. Luckily, she was standing inside of the screen door waiting for me, so I was able to scurry into the house, making my walk of shame short.

"*Girrrrrrl*, what in the fuck was you doin' with King *aaaaall* night?"

Urgh! Her voice sounded like nails on a chalkboard because my head was pounding. Even when she closed the door, my head felt like it wanted to pop.

"I told Siren to bring you home!"

I wish she had. "Well, she didn't," I told her as I slunk into the living room and plopped down on the couch.

I immediately laid down with my face on the pillows, but I felt Jada pulling on my arm.

"Unt uh! Hell nah! Get up and tell me what happened."

"Urgh," I groaned as Jada forcefully pulled my arm and sat me up. She looked at me with a smirk that told me that she already knew what had happened, but she just wanted to hear me say every single juicy detail. So, I sighed deeply, closed my eyes tight, and blurted out, "I fucked him."

"Oooo!" Her squeal was loud enough to wake up Dolla and her two kids, who were sleeping on the second floor. "Was it good?"

Was it good? Shiiid. "Hell yeah," I was sad to admit. "I saw the pearly gates. I saw Jesus Himself."

Jada fell out laughing, but I was so serious. Though it was short, and I only had one other man to compare him to, I had learned in those few minutes that King deserved his name because he had fucked me royally!

Finally, Jada stopped giggling to confront the look on my face. "What's wrong?"

"I'm embarrassed!"

Jada smirked as if I was being ridiculous. "Why?"

I looked at her like she was crazy. "Because I fucked him, and I don't even know him. I feel like a hoe."

"Girl, keep living," she chuckled with a dismissive wave of the hand. "That won't be the last time that you do some hoe shit."

"It will be if I can help it. He was just so...so... *sexy,* and I was so *drunk*. And I was so hurt about Reese."

"And King made it feel better, right?"

"For the moment," I admitted.

"So you got what you wanted. And ain't nothing wrong with that. Niggas do it all the time, girl," Jada replied, but it only made me feel a *little* bit better.

"It's still embarrassing. I don't want to keep seeing him, knowing that all he is thinking about is how I was some one-night stand."

Jada sucked her teeth and waved her hand again. "You won't be seeing him like that. I was surprised to see him out anyway. King is never on the block. I guess his fiancée really fucked his head up–"

My heart almost stopped. *"Fiancée?"*

Seeing my response, Jada suddenly looked like she had said too much.

"He has a *fiancée?" Oh my God. While I was so busy telling that man my life story, I hadn't once asked him his!*

"No, no! Not anymore," Jada quickly explained. "He left her at the altar when he overheard her on the phone talking to this nigga, Money. She had been fucking him all along. That was like two weeks ago."

"Two weeks?" My face fell into my hands.

"Yeah, but he is over her. Trust me. She was a dirty ass bitch. Siren and I got in that ass good. We were scrapping in bridesmaids dresses. That shit was funny." Jada laughed cynically while I marinated in my hoeism.

"Wait," I said looking her in the eyes. "That's the wedding that you'd been talking about being in?"

She nodded, and I cringed.

I couldn't believe it. This nigga was just at the altar two weeks ago, and now he was fucking me. Niggas ain't shit. No wonder he had called me another bitch's name: *Reina*. That shit don't sound anything like Kennedy.

"I was just some rebound pussy," I said, shaking my head.

"He was the same for you."

"True," I admitted with a deep sigh. "Well, it is what it is."

"Right. And there is nothing for you to be ashamed of. Tonight you did you. You had fun and ain't nothing wrong with that."

And that's all it was going to be: fun. My father was right. These hood niggas had an entourage of bitches, and I couldn't allow myself to become another notch on a nigga's belt. And it was obvious that that was all King wanted anyway. We had used each other. I hoped that King had enjoyed the few minutes that he got this pussy because I had no plans on giving him any more.

"Wait," I said remembering something. "Did Siren ever fuck King?"

"Hell nah," Jada replied immediately with a frown.

"You sure?"

"Yeah, why?"

"It seemed like it was some tension between them when he told her that he would take me home."

"I think she had a crush on him initially, but that was years ago. King has had a woman for a long time, and Siren would have told me if she was creeping with him." Then she shook her head confidently. "Hell nah."

KING

I was shocked as shit when I found myself actually thinking about shorty the next day. While I was sitting there on that couch, I only had intentions of banging her back out right then. But the moment I busted a nut, I was interested in at least, kicking it with her so that I could hit that again.

On the ride home, it was evident that she was regretting fucking me. Most women do after they sober up and realize that they had set that pussy out too fast. But it was obvious that shorty was just hurting. Shit, I was too. That's why I wanted to give her a call the next morning to let her know that it was okay and that I wanted to spend some more time with her to get to know her. But she just got out the car and slammed the door while I was asking for the digits. After walking out of that church, I never thought it was possible to even be interested in another chick, but there was an innocence about Kennedy that had a nigga intrigued. It was an innocence that I wanted to manipulate the hell out of ...in a good way.

I tried to shake thoughts of Kennedy when I heard Jay Z lyrics coming from the countertop in my kitchen where my cell was on the island.

♪ *So we live a life like a video where the sun is always out*
And you never get old, and the champagne's always cold

And the music is always good and the pretty girls

Just happen to stop by in the hood

And they hop they pretty ass up on the hood of that pretty ass car♪

That was the ringtone for my niggas, Meech and Dolla, so I knew it was one of them without even checking out the caller ID.

"Hello?"

"What up though?"

"What up, Dolla?"

"A lot, my nigga. I'm on my way to holla at you."

"Cool. I need to holla at you too. I need you to get Kennedy's number from Jada."

There was a slight pause for a few seconds. All I could hear was Rick Ross and the wind. Then Meech chuckled. "I knew you was feelin' shorty. Why didn't you get her number last night?"

A sneaky grin spread across my face as I thought back to that tight pussy. "I got more than that."

I could hear the humor and interest in his voice as he responded, "Oh word?"

"Yea, but I didn't get her number."

"How the fuck that happen?"

"Bro, who are you? The Feds with all these fucking questions?"

I was too embarrassed to tell him that she had rejected me when I asked for her number by slamming my car door in my face.

He chuckled again. "It's cool, bruh. Dolla'll tell me." And I knew he was right. I was sure that Kennedy went in that house and told Jada everything. And Jada was so in love with this nigga that she was going to pillow talk until her face hurt. But all of that was cool with me as long as I got Kennedy's number. "Get the digits for me, nigga. I'll see you in a minute."

With another chuckle, he replied, "Cool. One."

It only took ten minutes before I was receiving a text that included Kennedy's number. I had poured myself an afternoon shot of Jamo and was about to sit down in my recliner, take a sip, and call shorty when Dolla came through the door. For security and business purposes, he and Meech had keys to my crib, but only used them when they announced that they were coming or in emergency situations.

When I saw his face as he appeared in the doorway, I knew some shit had hit the fan. Meech was right behind him looking just as sick as Dolla was. They sat across from me on the couch with their eyebrows curled together with frustration. They were sweating like a motherfucka, but something told me that it wasn't just the summer sun that had them heated.

"What happened?"

Dolla let out a frustrated sigh before saying, "That nigga, Rozay, got popped yesterday with some werk."

Rozay worked for us. He was a younger dude, eighteen years old, that worked in our crew, selling werk in a higher quantity and weight than the younger niggas on the block.

"What they catch him with?"

"Like ten bricks," Meech answered.

I sat straight up. "Shit! Why am I just hearing about this?

Meech replied, "His girl just called me this morning. They didn't even give him a bond. This is his third strike."

"How'd he get caught?"

It looked like the color had left my dude's face as Dolla said, "Terry."

My face scrunched in confusion. Terry was a nobody-ass motherfucka who thought he was a dope boy. He copped weight on many occasions, but he never got to the level he wanted to because he couldn't stay out of the store spending his money on silly shit like Gucci, Rolexes, and other bullshit that attracted too much attention. He was a cool dude. We all knew each other from the hood and even broke bread together, but he was a goofy ass nigga that we stayed away from.

"Explain this shit to me, please."

With a deep breath, Meech laid it all out on the table. "Rozay's girl went to see his lawyer this morning. The lawyer say that nigga, Terry, been wearing a video wire. Apparently, he got into some shit and was facing some time. In exchange for his freedom, that nigga set Rozay up."

All my blood rushed to my head. The look on my face told Meech exactly what I was thinking, so he assured me, "She said that the lawyer promised that Rozay never said any names on the video. It was only him."

"But you know they pressin' him for names."

"Of course," Dolla agreed. "But I don't take Rozay as no snitch. He a young nigga, but he got a lot of heart. He's loyal as fuck."

"So let's show him how loyal we are and take care of that goofy ass nigga," I told them.

With a simple nod, Meech agreed.

"And since it's so much snitchin' going on, it might be something that we gotta handle ourselves," I ordered. "We can't trust nobody right now."

Dolla nodded as well. "Bet. Say no more."

August 2010

CHAPTER SEVEN

KING

It took us nearly over a month to find that goofy ass nigga, Terry. Of course, once Rozay was arrested, he fled the Chi, knowing that we would be after him for setting Rozay up. We couldn't put a manhunt out on him because we wanted this murder to be discreet and clean. The only people that knew about it were me, Meech and Dolla. Hell, we hadn't even put Rozay up on what we were doing. I just hired the best legal team to get him off or as little time as possible. He had sent word through his baby mama that the Feds were trying to get him to snitch, but he wasn't going to. He must have been telling the truth because, after a month, no cops had come knocking. For his loyalty, I kept hella money on his books and kept his entire family straight.

Meanwhile, I was going to handle his lightweight: Terry. As I said, after a month, he resurfaced in the Chi. His mother had had a stroke and died, and the funeral was on a Saturday morning in early August. We gave everyone a chance to say goodbye to Miss Judy before causing havoc. Me, Meech and Dolla sat across the street from the Gatling Funeral Home on 79th and Cottage Grove in a minivan that blended in nicely with the rest of the vehicles parked along the busy street.

As we sat and waited, thoughts of my pretty young thang ran across my mind. I had been calling Kennedy for a month with no answer. I didn't stalk her because I didn't want to scare her. I had probably called her three or four times over the past month. I'd even sent her a text message that had gone without a reply.

Shorty was rude as fuck. But the way that she was ignoring me was only making me want her that much more and further peaking my interest. The fact that she wasn't sweating me made me want to conquer her that much more. I had gone from wanting to fuck her again, to wanting to hang out with her, to wanting to date her. Something about the innocence and realness of our conversation that night had me yearning to have that same conversation with her over and over again. I wanted to spend that same kind of time with her when, except for Tiana, I had never been interested in such a thing. I was *King*. Every woman wanted to be with me. I didn't even have to ask for pussy. If I blinked, a bitch was on her knees giving me head. Yet, here this girl was playing games, and it was turning me the fuck on not only sexually, but emotionally.

"Here we go," I heard Meech say. I felt the minivan's engine start as I looked up and out of the back window. People were filing out of the funeral home doors. On cue, Dolla started the engine of the van while I found Terry in the crowd. He wasn't hard to find. Among a sea of family members dressed in all-white, I spotted Terry, third pallbearer on the right, carrying his mother toward the hearse.

"Let him put his moms in first," I ordered.

Meech and Dolla only nodded from the front seat, and I sat with my baretta in my lap. Usually, I didn't get my hands this dirty, but like I said, I needed this shit done and to stay under wraps. I had two cases against me already that I was dumb enough to catch in my teens. I hadn't caught a case since. No matter how young I was, I was smarter, wiser, and enjoyed my money and life way too much to get it taken away from me by a judge slapping thirty to life on my ass for a murder or drug conviction.

"A'ight," I said with a deep sigh after the hearse was closed. "Let's do this shit."

Without another word, the van began to slowly creep out of its parking space, giving me time to slide the door open. I was sure that I looked like the angel of death, dressed and masked in all black in front of so many people who were dressed like they should be singing in the heavenly choir. As I aimed, I saw fear coat a few faces. Just as I was spotted, screams rang out, but Terry wasn't as fast as the other people to run and cover.

Pow! Pow!

With two shots to the dome, he was on the ground, bleeding from the head behind the hearse. People scattered everywhere as Dolla sped off, and I slammed the door shut. I sat back in my seat, satisfied that I had taken care of business. Now it was time to take care of some other pressing matters.

KENNEDY

Hanging out with Jada and Siren had become a ritual. I had started school, but, after school and on the weekends, I was taking full advantage of the summer and my freedom. I was at Jada and Dolla's crib all the time, but I had been staying away from the block since fucking King. I was only going to clubs, malls, and what not with Jada and Siren, and avoiding any situations that I thought King might be in.

King had actually been calling me every now and then, but I wasn't trying to be some nigga's booty call on random nights. Reese had me so emotionally fucked up anyhow that I couldn't possibly see myself even dealing with a man at the time. I just wanted to have fun and focus on school.

Jada thought I was insane. "Are you crazy? Don't you know that every bitch in the hood wants that nigga's attention, and you got the nerve to be ignoring him?" That's what she was barking at me a week ago after King called again, and I ignored him.

"He don't want nothing," I said with a wave of the hand.

"Obviously, he does!"

"No, obviously he just wants some more ass, and I'm straight."

"Look, little girl; King don't sweat nobody, but he's sweating *you*. You need to call that man back."

I simply shook my head as I dug under my acrylic nails. "I'm straight, Jada."

In response, she rolled her eyes and shook her head like I was the dumbest bitch in the hood. "You're crazy as hell."

But she could think what she wanted to think. If I was being crazy, so be it, but at least I wasn't being used. However, she was the one that looked stupid as she barged into her bedroom one Saturday evening. As I lay on her bed watching reruns of *The Bad Girls Club*, the door swung open, and she appeared wide-eyed and with the goofiest look on her face.

"What?" I asked her as I sat up.

"Girl..." Her grin was so wide, and she looked like she was salivating with some juicy shit to say. "King is outside for you."

"Huh?!" Clearly, I hadn't heard her right.

She raced toward me. "*King is outside!*"

"For *me*?"

She sucked her teeth as she took my hand and begun to literally drag me out of bed. "Yes, for you!"

I was super confused as Jada pulled me into the hallway and toward the steps.

"What does he want?"

"I don't know, but you about to find out."

As Jada led me toward the front door by my one hand, I took my other hand and attempted to smooth out my hair. I was wearing it down in a long wrap. I was rocking a simple, coral, spaghetti strap maxi dress. It was August and hot as hell outside, so Jada and I were chilling in her house watching TV until the sun went down.

"Go!" Jada was forcing me out of the door as hesitation spread all over my face.

"He didn't say what he wanted?"

Jada blew her breath dramatically. "No! And it doesn't matter what he wants. King doesn't have to sweat nobody, but he has been sweating yo' ass! He's been calling you, and now he drove all the way over here to see you, so..." She paused as she swung the screen door open. "... Get yo' ass out there."

Shit, at this point, I had to go see what he wanted if I wanted Jada to shut the hell up. So, reluctantly, I walked out onto the porch and laid my eyes on a vision that reminded me why I had given my pussy up so easily. King was so gawd damn fine. There is no other way to describe him. Standing in that driveway and leaning against that Camaro made him look like the vision that I imagined how every thug would look in the novels that I read at night. He was book-perfect. He had the type of attractiveness that was unbelievable and that could only be created in someone's imagination. I was weak in the knees as I attempted to sashay toward him like his visit meant nothing.

"Sooo, I gotta basically stalk you to get you to talk to me?" The way that he was smirking with that gorgeous, endearing smile made all of my reluctance and stubbornness immediately wash away like it was never there. A smile spread across my face as he asked, "Why don't you want to talk to me?"

I had all kinds of reasons, but as I finally came two feet away from him, he walked up on me and took me by the hand. I was speechless.

"What's up, ma? I thought we had a good time that night."

Say something. But I couldn't as long as I was looking into those pretty ass eyes, so I focused on the street and watched the cars go by as I forced words to leave my throat. "We did have a good time."

"So what's the problem?"

"It's not a problem. We hung out. We had a good time. That's it."

"That's it?" He sounded so shocked that I looked at him, surprised that it sounded like he was hurt. "That wasn't it for me."

My lips parted a few times, but I couldn't figure out what to say. Who wouldn't want to do whatever with this man? Fuck him, love him, spit shine his shoes! But on the other hand, I wasn't ready for how he made me feel when he was near me. He was so damn intimidating to the point that I wanted to run from him. And let's not forget, I was too hurt and untrusting to deal with another hustler, their female baggage, and mind games.

I was sure that all of that reluctance was written all over my face because he pulled me closer to him, saying, "I wanna take you out and spend some time with you. We don't have to have sex."

94

It was crazy to me that he actually looked sincere, so for the first time since stepping outside I was assertive because I needed to know. "Why do you want to spend time with me?"

As I said, I needed to know. He was a grown ass man with money and status. Here I was some little ass girl compared to him, with no experience with anything in life. And he wanted to spend time with me? I didn't get it.

"Because I'm digging you."

I shook my head in disbelief as I kept trying to avoid those eyes and that smile. "You don't even know me."

"I'm trying to, Reina."

"See?!" My hands flew into the air with frustration. "You don't even know my name!"

When he smiled and chuckled, it pissed me the fuck off. Here he was, fronting like he was feeling me, but the motherfucker didn't even know my name! I was offended as fuck, so turned to leave, but he quickly wrapped his arms around my waist. And with that man's arms around me, at the moment, I didn't give a fuck what name he called me.

"No, sweetheart, Reina means queen in Spanish." His breath brushed right against my ear, causing me to shiver right there in the driveway. "It's fitting to call you that since I'm trying to make you my queen."

Dumbfounded was an understatement. I was speechless and so fucking turned on.

"Now," he said, pausing as he let me go. I was actually sad that I was no longer in his arms. Then he opened the passenger side door of the Camaro. "Would you please get in the car so that we can go eat?"

I caught a glimpse of Jada in the window, doing a very poor job of being discreet. When I saw the smile on her face, I thought maybe I should stop running from him. Maybe he wouldn't hurt me like Reese. And maybe...*just maybe*... since he was being so persistent, King might have been meant to be. So I let go of my inhibitions and climbed into the car.

On the way to the restaurant, we actually got to know each other some more. We were so drunk the first time that we'd hung out that we both had forgotten a few things that we talked about that night.

Even though I had hung with him that night, after hearing Jada go on and on about him almost every day since, I had grown intimidated by him. In my mind, he was the rich, distant, and a feared man that everyone told me that he was. But during the drive, I was reminded that he was actually surprisingly humble, laid back, cool as hell, and never missed a moment to make me laugh. He cracked continuous jokes about how I had him chasing me.

We were so busy laughing and talking that, before I knew it, he was pulling into the valet area of a restaurant. The huge bright sign on the building read Pearl's, and I noticed that we were in

Bronzeville, one of the more cultural, upscale communities on the South Side of Chicago. Through the picture windows, I could see that the fairly large- sized restaurant was full of patrons from upper-class African Americans to the CTA drivers that had just gotten off of work, to the thugs. They were all piled in. Every table was full, and the bar was packed.

I was taken aback when King left the car and circled it to open my door. Then he took my hand, helping me out of the car, and continued to hold my hand as he handed his keys to the valet driver. Then he led us toward the restaurant. I can't lie. I had butterflies in my stomach, and I was reminded why I had been avoiding this nigga. He truly had the presence of a king, and I felt like a mere, young peasant standing next to him in his shadow.

I felt even lower when I noticed the sign on the door. "King," I called his name as my pace slowed. "I can't go in there. I'm not twenty-one."

He looked back at me, smiled, and urged me to follow him. "It's fine. C'mon."

But I saw the mean-looking bouncers at the door and insisted. "No, King. I don't want to be embarrassed when they card me."

"It's cool. You'll be fine. I know the owner." Then he released my hand and extended his as if he was waiting to shake mine. "Meet the owner."

That damn smile of his could talk me into doing anything. Little did I know that it would. That smile, his presence, would change my life like I never knew it would.

JADA

I was still laughing into the phone as Siren answered, "Hello?"

I was giggling uncontrollably. "Hey, girl," I said, as I sat on the couch flipping through channels. I couldn't believe this shit.

"What's so funny?"

"*Girrrl*, you would not believe what I just saw."

"What?" she asked excitedly, ready for some gossip.

"So King has been stalking the shit out of Kennedy."

"What?"

"Yes, girl. He's been on her bumper since the day they met at the spot." I purposely left out the fact that Kennedy had given King some. That was her business to tell, and if he ended up wifing her like he planned, it would be obvious anyway.

"Humph," Siren grunted.

"I know, right? That's so not like King. He didn't even sweat Tiana, and she and King were engaged! I can't believe it. The nigga acts like he's smitten. He made me give him her number and actually kept calling after she was blatantly ignoring his calls."

"Ignoring his calls?"

"Yes! Can you believe that? She felt like he was just trying to get some ass, which would be a typical nigga move. But I told her that King don't sweat nobody. He def wouldn't have been calling her back after she didn't return the first call." I lay back on the couch with my legs propped up on the pillow and my cell cradled between my ear and shoulder, just running my mouth without a care in the world. "But not only did he keep calling... You ain't gon' believe this."

"What? What? Tell me!"

"He *shooowed* up at my house a few minutes ago. Basically, he made the girl get in the car with him. He wasn't playin' no games! It was like a hood fairy tale. It was *sooo* cute!" I was expecting Siren to gag along with me, but I heard nothing but the television in the background. "Hello? Siren?"

"Yeah, Jada, let me call you back."

"What's wro–"

When it seemed as if her end of the line went dead, I thought, *The hell?* I looked at my screen and, sure enough, the call had ended. *The hell is wrong with her?*

I didn't think twice about it. *Maybe her signal dropped.* I shrugged my shoulders as I grabbed the remote, still wearing the same teasing smile. I was so happy for Kennedy and King. My cousin deserved to finally be with a real nigga after what Reese did to her. I also knew that Kennedy's intelligence and ambition would be a good change for King. Plus with me being in a relationship with his best friend, it would be so cool if King dated my cousin.

I thought it was going to be just perfect.

Present day

Release day

Chapter Eight

Kennedy

King and I didn't spend the night in the hotel.

"I want to go home, baby," I whispered, barely able to catch my breath after we'd had sex for the third time. Our eyes were heavy, and sweat pooled on the surface of our skin as the sun rose. I was tired from the long, exciting day, but I just couldn't sleep.

"You sure?" he asked.

I looked around that beautiful, exquisite suite and let out a deep sigh. The environment was beautiful and romantic, but it wasn't what I had fantasized about for the last three years.

"Yeah, I'm sure. I want to lay in my own bed with you and my baby. She's home, right?"

King sat up on his elbows, his skin looking amazing against the rising sun that reflected off of him through the picture window. "Yeah, she's with the nanny."

I smiled, the thought of my daughter brought a warm and fuzzy feeling to my heart.

"Then c'mon," King told me as he bent over and kissed my lips. "Let's go home."

We got dressed quickly, and we rode hand-in-hand all the way home. I stared out of the window at every single thing. Some parts of the city had changed so much, and I was taking it all in. Then when we pulled into a gated community, I was in awe. Inside of the gates looked like Mayberry, not the South Suburbs. King had the biggest smile on his face as my eyes grew to the size of golf balls. During calls and visits, he told me that he had upgraded, but he never showed me pictures or went into details, saying that he wanted it all to be a surprise when I got out. And I was definitely surprised when King pulled the car into the circle driveway of a mansion!

"Oh my God, King! This is beautiful!" I was fighting to get out of the car. I was so frantic that I couldn't get the simple lock to open. King chuckled as I stumbled out of the car before he could even make it to my side to open the car door for me.

The single family, three-bedroom home that we were living in on the South Side when I went to jail was absolutely no comparison to the ten-thousand square foot red brick home that was towering over me.

I was squealing and giggling as I ran up the driveway toward the door. King was right behind me, chuckling in satisfaction with my happiness. As always, he was happy because I was happy. When he slid his key into the lock and opened the door, my eyes filled with tears. The happiness wasn't vanity because the house was so beautiful. It was because, in the blink of an eye, I had gone from being surrounded by concrete walls to being surrounded by the most exquisitely decorated home that I had only previously seen in magazines.

"Damn, is that suede?" I ran up to the wall and touched the paint curiously. "It doesn't feel like suede."

"It's a suede paint that makes the walls *look* suede."

"Damn, that's nice," I said nearly in a whisper.

Downstairs was a kitchen engineered for the finest chef and a living room big enough for the three of us to live in. And I was sure that King, Meech, and Dolla had taken over the den on many nights watching games or fights. Off of the kitchen was a deck with the most comfortable looking outdoor furniture. I couldn't wait to grab a glass of wine and a book and just sit out there with nothing but the sun and the massive trees that populated the huge yard.

There were five bedrooms upstairs. Three were guest bedrooms, each with a private bathroom.

"Oooo!" I squealed quietly as we tiptoed into Kayla's room. The décor made her room look like a castle, including a princess castle, pink and purple loft bed. I wasn't surprised to see the theme since Kayla was King's princess.

Tears were still flowing as I scooped Kayla out of her bed. I had had a wonderful time that night. The entire day was like a dream, but now, all I wanted to do was hold both of my babies, King and Kayla. So with Kayla in my arms, I followed King inside of the bedroom next to hers. It was the master suite. Once again, my breath was taken away. The room was the size of the massive living room downstairs. The beautiful bed was calling my name. In the corner was a sofa set that matched the one downstairs.

I won't ever have to leave this room if I don't want to.

There was a Jacuzzi in the master bathroom that I made a special, private date with for the next day. God, it had been so long since I was able to soak my body in hot water and bubbles, and I couldn't fucking wait!

There was marble tile from floor to ceiling. I truly felt like I was in quarters fit for royalty. I looked back at my King, and he was wearing the most satisfied smile on his face. I stood on my tiptoes and kissed him softly, and as I did, Kayla squirmed in her sleep.

"Lay her down," he whispered. "I have something else to show you."

I couldn't imagine what other surprise my man had up his sleeve, but I was ready to see what it was. King knew that my life was taken away from me simply because I'd met him, and he was repaying me in any way that he could.

This house was a good damn start! But the house also showed me how much King's business had tripled since I went away. He was no longer supplying a few local dope boys with bricks. He was moving major weight across the state and even states surrounding us and had set up an operation down south.

Picture windows covered most of the walls, so I glanced through one as I walked by toward the bed. My eyesight fell upon a stunning 570-square-foot terrace with a gazebo. *Gawd damn! Nigga, we made it!*

I was still slowly moving, taking in every detail of my new home carefully, but King was behind me, hurrying me because he couldn't wait to show me what was next. I carefully laid Kayla down and as soon as I did, King took my hand in his and led me through the bedroom toward the door in the far corner. I knew that something special was inside because King couldn't stop cheesing.

"Ta da!" he whispered as he flung the door open with a huge grin that was so corny. As I laid eyes on what was inside, I fell in love with the man all over again. My love wasn't because he had filled the walk-in closet with hundreds of thousands of dollars' worth of designer clothes, shoes, jewelry, and handbags. It was because he had taken the time to make sure that I had everything that I would want and need as soon as I stepped foot out of those gates. Everything that I had fantasized about during our calls and visits was given to me as soon I arrived. He had been so careful that he didn't miss a detail. And that's why he would always have my love and loyalty.

KENNEDY

We finally fell asleep around seven in the morning. But a mere four hours later, King received a text message that brought us out of our sleep. After he read it, he jumped out of bed.

"It's urgent," he quickly told me. "I gotta go meet up with Meech and Dolla. I'll be back."

I was too sleepy to ask any questions, so I just threw the covers back over me and Kayla after he kissed me goodbye and tried to fall back to sleep.

Then, not five minutes after King left, Kayla woke up.

"Where's Daddy? I want my Daddy!" She was screaming with fear in her eyes, and I saw the onset of a full-blown hysterical cry coming on.

I sat up and reached for her. "It's okay, baby. Daddy isn't here."

When she pulled away from me, I was shocked. When she started to wail, and I focused on the horror in her eyes, I remembered; she didn't know me. Just as that realization made me cringe, her wails became even louder and more piercing.

Shit. I attempted to calm her down, but it was impossible when a complete anxiety attack was running toward me like a freight train. Here I was, alone with my daughter, and she didn't even know me. Every time I went to hug her, rub her back, or run my fingers through her hair, she just continued to cry and pulled away from me, which made me cry just as hard as she was.

"I'm sorry, Kayla. I'm sorry." I probably shouldn't have been crying in front of her. Surely, it wasn't helping the situation any, but the tears continued to pour out every time she looked at me like she had no clue who the hell I was. I had been so ride or die for King, but I had forgotten about the only person on this earth that mattered more to me than him: my daughter. I'd left her out here, knowing that her father would take care of her, but too young and dumb to realize that in the process she would forget all about me.

I sat on the bed with tears streaming down my face as Kayla cried uncontrollably. She wouldn't listen to anything that I said. If I tried to hold her, she fought me. When she tried to leave out of the closed bedroom door, and I stopped her, she pulled away and cried even more.

The screaming didn't bother me. After a few weeks of being in prison, I had learned how to block out unwanted noises and voices. I was able to tune her out, but the face of a daughter that didn't know me, I couldn't ignore.

Thankfully, my phone rang, and it was Jada.

"Hello?"

"Kennedy?" She fought to hear me over Kayla's screams in my background. Her voice was laced with the curiosity of what the hell was going on. "Are you crying? What's wrong?"

"She doesn't know me," I cried.

Sympathy was all over her words as she replied, "Oh God. I'm sorry, Kennedy. But she'll get used to you. Where is the nanny?"

"I told King to give her a few days off so that I could be alone with Ka—"

Blood-curdling screams left Kayla's throat so staggering that I jumped.

"Oh shit," I heard Jada say.

"I don't know what to do." I was whining so much that I probably sounded just like Kayla. "Would you come over, please?" I asked Jada, nearly begging as I wiped the tears from my eyes.

"Sure. I'm on my way."

KING

I slid into Meech's driveway at record speed. He had also upgraded over the years, having moved himself and Siren into a phat ass crib a few miles away from my mansion in Country Club Hills. He no longer lived in that apartment on the East Side of the Chi. This shit was lavish, and a reflection of the constant come up that we had been on while Kennedy was gone.

I hopped out of the car and ran through the plush, green grass, straight to the front door and through it. Meech and Dollar were sitting in the living room waiting for me.

"The fuck is going on?" I'll admit I was scared. Meech and Dolla knew that, since Kennedy was out, I wanted some free time with her. I wasn't to be disturbed unless it was an emergency, and emergency meant life or death. Meech and Dolla had grown from my two right-hand men to business partners, so they knew how to take care of any mishaps in the system without me. So when I got the "911" text from Meech, my antennas went up immediately. We didn't have emergencies in our empire. We were paying off enough cops and politicians to keep the Feds off of us. They hadn't tried to take us down since the punk ass nigga, Terry, set Rozay up. Murders and thefts were a rare occurrence because we didn't just have some little young teenage wannabes selling dope out of trap houses in the hood anymore. We ran an organization that was well-built on respect that sold weight to hustlers so high up on the food chain that the next nigga buying it from him didn't know who the fuck we were.

I walked through Meech's crib eyeing him and Dolla curiously. They looked sick to their stomachs, and I didn't like that shit at all. In over five years of working side by side with them, I had rarely seen fear in their eyes. I was seeing it now, and that shit had me on edge.

"What's up?" I asked again as I sat on Meech's couch.

After taking a deep breath, Dolla spoke up. "A detective pulled me over after I left the crib early this morning. I just knew that she was going to search my ride, but instead she started asking questions about Terry's murder."

Awkward silence and weird tension filled the air. The only three people that knew about Terry's murder were the nigga sitting to my right and the one sitting across from me. I looked over at Dolla asking, "What kind of questions?"

He was so scared that he was mumbling and couldn't even look me in the eyes. "Where was I that day? How did I know Terry? Have I ever driven a black minivan?" Dolla explained.

"And then what?"

"I was short-lipped with the shit because it was odd; she didn't take me into the station or shit. When I wasn't giving her the answers that she wanted, she let me go but said that she'd be back."

I hid my own fear. The police obviously knew very specific details about that day that only people that were there should know.

Meech let out a deep sigh as he sat across from us in a loveseat clutching a glass of vodka. The tension grew more and more. I didn't give a fuck about how much drugs we sold or how big of an organization we ran. Nobody wanted to go jail for murdering a state's witness. We'd never see the free world again.

"How would they know to come talk to me?" Dolla had directed that question at me, and it threw both me and Meech the fuck off. We first shot curious expressions at each other before looking at Dolla like he had lost his mind.

I sat up and turned to look him straight in the eye. "What the fuck you mean by that, bruh?"

"I'm saying, though..." He was saying something, but he knew better than to look me in my fucking eyes when he said it. He looked at Meech's hickory hardwood floors as he continued, "Nobody knew about this shit but *us*. I know you talk to your girl about everything, and she got out early. You think she–"

Before he could finish his motherfucking sentence, I had snatched my piece from my waist and had it pointed at his motherfucking temple.

"King!" Meech shouted in a threatening tone as his eyes bulged. "C'mon, bro! Chill out!"

Dolla sat extra still, facing forward, not a muscle moving as I tensed up on the trigger, coaxing him. "Now, what the fuck was you sayin'?"

"He wasn't saying shit, man." Meech was begging for this nigga's life more than he was.

Granted, the two niggas in the room were the only other people in this world that I loved more than Kennedy and Kayla. Hell, I probably loved them more than I loved myself. Many times, I had made sure that they and their families were straight before me and my own. They were also the two people that were out there getting money because of the sacrifice that Kennedy had made. So no matter how deep that love was, I'd kill a motherfucka for talking against my Reina. Dolla knew that. Every motherfucking body who knew *us* knew *that*. So the fact that he would fix his fucking mouth to imply that shit meant that he really fucking believed it.

"King!" Meech was calling my name as I stared at Dolla, jaw clinched, gun still to his head and his eyes still to the ground. "King!"

Dolla actually had the nerve to turn and look me in my eyes. "Bruh, they came to question *me*. Why?"

Meech interrupted him, continuing to plead for him to be quiet and save his own life. "Shut the fuck up, Dolla!"

But he continued as I bit my lip and aimed directly in the middle of his eyes. "Nobody knew shit. We got rid of the van. We got rid of the burners."

"Dolla!" At that point, Meech had stood up as if that would get our attention. "Man, *shut up!*"

"Yeah, nigga, we did all that. So we good," I told him. "That's probably the one thing that I never told Kennedy." That revelation made Dolla relax, and Meech was satisfied that I had showed Dolla that he was wrong, but I was still pissed and aiming at his skull. "I love you like a brother, but I will kill yo' motherfuckin' ass if you come against my girl like that again."

I put the gun away with a heavy heart, but I still respected Dolla. And when we looked in each other's eyes, I knew that he still respected me too. He had said what he had to say, and I had done what I needed to do. At the end of the day, we would still be fam and getting this money.

KENNEDY

As soon as Jada walked through the door, Kayla ran to her, and the tantrum ceased automatically.

Tears quietly rolled down my cheeks as I watched my child embrace another woman like she was her mother and not me. It was obvious that I hadn't been there to nurture Kayla, to make her feel safe, to love on her. It was painfully obvious that my cousin and friends had had to step up to the plate to replace the mother that Kayla was forced to miss for the last few years.

"She'll get used to you," Jada assured me. But that didn't make me feel any better. "Get dressed. Let's get out of here."

"I don't feel like going anywhere," I whined with my lip slightly poked out.

Jada sucked her teeth, locked her arm in mine and started walking toward the staircase. "C'mon, girl. You've been locked up long enough," she fussed, pushing me up the stairs. "I'm not going to let you just sit around the house. It'll be okay. She'll figure out that you're her mother in no time."

I gave in and went into my bedroom to get dressed while Jada took Kayla into her bedroom to get her dressed. Jada was right. Before I went away, I wasn't some sad, depressed or defeated chick, and I wasn't about to be that now. Honestly, once I walked into that big ass walk-in closet, I felt a hell of a lot better with all of those labels staring back at me. Three years ago, I knew nothing about Hermes, Giuseppe, Herve or Red Bottoms. Before I was arrested, I was a kid, not even twenty-one. Back then, I thought Apple Bottoms were the shit. When King bought me my first Coach purse, I cried. Now, his money had advanced to such lengths that I was gifted a closet full of clothes with price tags that looked more like bank account balances than prices.

After showering, I slipped on an Alice + Olivia maxi dress. The airy cotton maxi dress with a handkerchief hem was beautiful and made my figure look amazing. The lace detailing made me look more romantic and less like a felon.

Damn, this is nice, but it's way too expensive. He's spending too much money. I eyed the price tag as I cut it off. It was over nine hundred dollars, which was way too much for my taste. Hell, a damn cotton maxi from Akira would have been okay with me compared to where I had just come from.

I paired the white dress with a pair of black Giuseppe stiletto sandals, which matched the lace on the dress. After throwing a few barrel curls in my extensions and putting on a little makeup, I was walking out of the master bedroom just as Jada was walking out of Kayla's room holding her hand. My baby looked so pretty that I instantly blushed.

"Look at you, Kayla," I cooed, and she instantly stepped back and wrapped her arms around Jada's legs tightly, as if she was afraid of me. It was like I was some big, bad monster or some shit.

I sucked my teeth. "Oh, forget you, lil' girl," I snarled, as I waved her off. Jada fell out laughing.

After climbing into Jada's truck, we headed to Pappadeaux for lunch.

"Where is Siren?" I asked Jada. "We should have asked her to come with us."

"I did. She was stuck with Elijah, though."

I sucked my teeth and shook my head. It was fucked up that Elijah's father was never around. He was this guy from out west that Siren was messing with at the time she got pregnant. When she found out that she was pregnant, he pulled the typical ain't-shit-nigga move and bounced because he wasn't ready to be a father. He wanted Siren to have an abortion. When she refused, he decided not to be a part of Elijah's life. His disappearing act often caused Siren to miss outings like this with her girls.

"Did King mention to you what was going on?"

"No," I told Jada. "He jumped up and ran out of the house this morning. He checked in while I was getting dressed, but he didn't say anything, and I didn't ask," I explained. "Did Dolla say anything to you? I'm sure they're together."

"No, but he disappeared for a few hours this morning. He wouldn't even answer the phone. Then just showed up at the crib looking like he'd seen a damn ghost or something."

"Humph," was all that I muttered.

"I'm going to call Siren to see if Meech told her anything."

I was only a day and a half out of prison, and there was already some shit. But whatever it was, I was sure that King would keep it as far away from me as possible in order to spare me from any trouble. Although I was the one who'd been locked up, he had lived with the guilt the entire time that I was gone. He would never allow that to happen to me again, and he would do anything in his power to prevent it, including keeping me completely out of the loop.

"*Sooo...*"

I looked reluctantly at Jada, knowing that her slow drawl meant that bullshit was to follow. She met my eyes with a smirk, confirming that it was. "I called your father today."

"Fuck," I sighed as I ran my fingers through my hair.

"Oooo!" Kayla's voice came screeching from the backseat. "You not 'posed to say fuck."

"Kayla!" Jada warned her.

But she just went on like it was nothing. "Dat's a bad word. Jada, charge her five dollars."

My eyes bucked as Jada laughed.

I rolled my eyes, asking, "Who taught her that?"

"King doesn't curse around her. She doesn't like bad words. If anyone of us slips, we have to give her five dollars."

I sucked my teeth as I reached in my pocket. Pulling out the wad of cash that King had left me with that morning, I pulled off a hundred dollar bill and handed it to Kayla. "I'm gon' be doing a lot of cursing if I have to talk about my father."

Jada started cracking up.

But I didn't find shit funny. "Why would you call *him*?"

"Because y'all need to talk. For real. You should go see him."

Again, I sucked my teeth. "Why? He doesn't want to see me! He didn't even answer my calls while I was locked up!" Just the thought of it hurt like hell. Many days I had sat by that phone, listening to my calls go unanswered and feeling like that scared little girl that just wanted to talk to her daddy.

"You both have been stubborn since that day."

My mouth dropped. "*Me*? I tried to call him!"

"You didn't try hard enough, and you know it."

I sighed deeply and didn't bother arguing back. She was right. Although I had tried calling while I was locked up, it was only a few times. And I had given up last year after listening to his voicemail yet again.

Once arriving at Pappadeaux, we went straight to the restroom to wash our hands before being seated. Kayla was still holding on to Jada for dear life, so she followed Jada into the stall. While in the stall, I replied back to text messages from my mother. I was setting up a time to see her soon. I had refused to let her visit me in prison as well. I was ashamed. I loved King to death, but I knew that I had ultimately disappointed my parents, especially my father. Having my mother come see me behind those walls would have made the last three years even worse.

"Hey, Jada! Hey, Kayla!" The female voice tore my attention away from my text messages; especially when she spoke to my daughter like she knew her personally. I hurried out of the stall just in time to see a tall, light skin, slim-thick chick smiling all up in Jada's face. "Where is King?" she asked and Jada's eyes got wide. "I heard his bitch got out of prison."

Jada's mouth opened, but before she could warn this goofy bitch, I stepped right in between them. "Yeah, his bitch did get out of prison. Hi, *I'm* that bitch."

Jada instantly grabbed Kayla's hand and pulled her back as I watched the sorrowful expression on this bitch's face with little sympathy. Instantly, she regretted every word she had said, but her apologetic expression wasn't enough.

Nobody fucked with my family; not the police and definitely not some goofy bitch asking about my man with the wrong agenda.

"It's in your best interest not to ask about King anymore unless yo' nigga into buying some weight. And by the looks of that regular ass weave in your head, you don't fuck with niggas of that caliber."

"Bi–"

As soon as I stepped into her face with the look of terror in my eyes, I stopped whatever threats she thought she wanted to make. I was sure that I was going a bit overboard, but that's what I had been taught to do to survive. "You know, I never *want* to go back jail. But what doing time taught me is that I *can* do the time. It didn't kill me, so I *will* do it again when it comes to my man or my family. Let's make that crystal clear." Then I put my finger to her forehead and pushed. "Don't ask about him again, bitch."

She stumbled a bit, but my eyes dared her to make a move. She didn't. She knew better. She just sucked her teeth and walked out with Jada's cackling laughter playing as her exiting soundtrack.

I had been gone for a long time, and King was a nigga. I knew better than to think that the nigga had been using his hand all this time, although he swore he had been faithful. Either way, these bitches were about to find out that Mrs. Damion "King" Carter was back, and I wasn't dealing with these money, status hungry bitches. I was sure that little heifer was about to run and tell everybody.

"Daaamn! Whooosaaa! Shit!" Jada continued to laugh as she washed her hands. "Relax, ma. You ready to kick a bitch's ass. Slow down, GI Jane."

She was too busy laughing and washing her hands to see that I was fighting to make my anger subside. That shit wasn't funny. She didn't know the things I had to do to survive while locked up with them bitches. She should've been praying to God that she would never be faced with the decision to have to turn her back on her man or herself and find out the hard way.

JADA

"Brittany and Brandon, go upstairs. I need to talk to your mother."

I wasn't surprised when Brandon sucked his teeth in protest. He was a kid, and his father was stopping him right in the middle of his Xbox game. "Dad, c'mon. I'm almost done."

I stopped folding the towels and looked at him like he was crazy. "Listen to your father, Brandon. I told you about playing that game in my living room anyway. You have a TV and a system in your room. Go upstairs."

"But ma–"

"*Now!*"

Brittany, my oldest, laughed at him mockingly as she followed a pouting Brandon up the stairs. My kids were eight and seven. I had had them back-to-back during junior and senior year of high school. We were young when we had them, but Dolla and I both were happy that we'd had them then and not later. There was way too much going on in our lives now to be chasing after some toddlers in diapers as well.

"What's up, baby?" I didn't even bother looking at him as I continued to fold the towels. Since he'd made the kids leave, I figured that he wanted to talk about some shit that had to do with the business. But when he grabbed my hand to make me give him my undivided attention, I knew it was serious, so I put the towel in my hand to the side. "What's wrong?"

He sat beside me with his eyebrows curled up in frustration. "Did you talk to anybody about that murder we did a few years back?"

I sucked my teeth. "Boy, are you crazy? You know I know better than that."

"Not anybody? Not even *Siren*?"

"Hell no!"

"I'm serious, Jada."

"I'm serious too! Don't come at me like that. I've been with you for years, so I know how the game goes. I wouldn't even repeat no shit like that! Don't insult me!" I was heated. If anything, Dolla knew how loyal I was. I wasn't just his girlfriend or baby mama. I had been deep in the game with his ass since day one. He, King, and Meech were the masterminds behind all of this shit, but as Dolla's woman and his rider, I had implicated myself in so much shit that I could be put away for a lot of years if shit ever went down. He had taught me well. I was too smart to run my mouth, and he should have known that.

But as I recognized the fear in his eyes, my anger shifted to concern. "What's wrong?"

He instantly answered, "Nothing," but I knew he was full of shit.

With a deep sigh, I said, "Dolla..." I paused, trying to manage my anger. I knew my man, and I knew better than to take this shit personal because obviously some shit was fucking with him that had nothing to do with me. But the motherfucker was getting on my nerves. "Talk to me. We've been in this shit together for years. Meech and King are your partners, but, as your woman, so am I. You've never lied to me, so don't start lying now. You ran up outta this motherfucker this morning without explaining yourself. You were missing for hours yesterday. What's going on?"

When Dolla threw his face in his hands, I got scared. The longer he sat slumped over like that, with his elbows resting on his knees, I got more and more nervous. "*Dolla*," I begged.

"I got questioned about Terry's murder this morning."

At that moment, my heart began to quake. Despite the business that they were in, King, Meech, and Dolla were smart about every move they made. It wasn't just to keep them out of jail. They loved their women and families enough to protect us from experiencing the hurt of burying them or visiting them in a prison. They had only dropped the ball once, and that was when Kennedy got arrested. And to this day, no one has been able to figure out how that happened.

"W-what d-did they say?" This shit had me so shook that I was stuttering.

"They asked some routine questions about how I knew Terry." He had revealed his face again, but he was so scared that he couldn't even look me in the eyes.

"But-but they let you go, so obviously they don't have that much evidence. Right?"

"Right. But why after five years would they come straight to *me*? Somebody snitched."

"Do you have any idea who?" I lay my hand on his back and started to rub soothingly, attempting to erase his fear and mine.

"Not a clue," he admitted. "Nobody knew. We were careful."

"Well, you told me. You think...?"

"Meech wouldn't tell Siren no shit like that, and I asked King if maybe Kennedy told–"

My gasp interrupted him. "Dolla, you didn't!"

"Well, shit, I had to ask. She got out early."

"For *good behavior*!" I insisted as I slapped his arm. "How could you even imply that shit?"

Again, Dolla threw his face in his hands. "I had to ask. It's the only way."

"And what did King say?"

"After he put a gun to my head?" My jaw dropped to the carpet as he continued. "He said that he never even told her, and I believe him."

"I can believe that too. He protects that girl from everything. Well, he tries to anyway."

February 2011

CHAPTER NINE

KENNEDY

If angels wear Vicki's and the devil wears Prada, I guess I was a taste of heaven and hell back then because King had completely turned Daddy's little angel into a hell of a rider. I was every definition of *his girl*, and I absolutely loved it.

"Shit, baby," I breathed heavily into King's ear. "Yes. Right there. Fuck me."

By February of 2011, King and I had been together for six months, and we were every bit of a couple.

"Grrr," he growled into my ear as he lay on top of me giving me the best dick of my life. "*Fuck*, this pussy know it's tight. I love this pussy, ma."

"It loves you too. It's yours, baby," I promised him. And I wasn't lying.

While I initially thought that King would only treat me like a piece of pussy, for the past six months, he had treated me like the total opposite. He had treated me like his queen.

Our first date at the restaurant was surprisingly the most fun I'd ever had in my life. Even though he was the owner, we sat at the bar and mingled. To my surprise, despite his cool, quiet demeanor, King was a social butterfly. He was down to earth, and not the stuck up nigga with the money. No one would have known who he really was because he treated everybody with the respect that they should have been giving him. I was so turned on by how humble he was and, though a street nigga, how smart he was. He was not just a drug dealer; he was an astute businessman. When I talked about school, he cared and listened. He was impressed with how passionate I was about child psychology and he was actually familiar with some of the issues and disorders that most African-American children faced.

I was even further surprised when he didn't try to fuck that night. We talked and laughed until, unbeknownst to us, everyone in the restaurant was gone, and it was closed. Then he dropped me off at Jada's house, promising to call me the next day. But he actually called that night, and we talked until five in the morning.

We hung out every other day for the first two months. He would pick me up after class, and we would tear the city apart. Every now and then, we would both say that we could not believe how much we liked each other. He had been heartbroken, and so had I, but the walls around our hearts came crashing down every time we hung out.

We got along great. Our age difference was a non-existent issue. We kept each other laughing, and the sex was off the chain! King had taught this virgin how to fuck a grown ass man. And honestly, I didn't mind it at all, because, in the short time that I had known King, he had made me feel happier and more loved than Reese had in a year. That's why, a month after our date, I made him take this pussy. He had been more than a gentleman, showing me that it was about more than sex by not asking, but one night at his house, I decided I had waited long enough. By then, everyone in the hood knew that I was his, even without the title, because he kept me by his side. Since he was the head of his organization, he had a lot of free time on his hands, so we spent days hanging out at the lake front and parties with Meech, Dolla, Jada, and Siren. We also spent quiet evenings alone at his house.

Four months ago, he surprised me. He told Jada to drop me off at his house. When I walked in, I was called into the kitchen. My breath was taken away when I walked into an abundance of the most beautiful roses. They were everywhere. There were so many that I hardly recognized the kitchen. King was standing next to the kitchen table that was set for two. At the stove was an older, black guy dressed as a chef. I was so shocked and touched that I was speechless. Though I had only dated two men in my short life, no one had ever done anything so sweet with solely me in mind.

We were eating the salad and appetizers when he put his fork down onto his plate and held my hand. "I want you to be my woman *officially*."

The biggest smile spread across my face because to be King's woman was an honor. Not just because of his money and street status either. Outside of the tattoos, rough exterior, and dope boy swag was a *man*. He treasured me like I was his prized possession. I never thought or worried about other women because he always made me feel like I was the only woman on his mind.

"Sure," I smiled. "I'd love to be your queen, King."

Though I was for it, he looked hesitant, and I watched curiously because it looked like he was trying to find the right words to say.

"What's wrong?" I asked as I squeezed his hand.

"Bae, I just want you to be sure. Being with me comes with a lot of responsibility. I'll try to keep my business away from you as much as possible to protect you, but you need to know who I am."

"What do you mean? I know who you are. I know what you do."

"But I'm not just some nigga selling ounces to petty drug dealers in the hood, baby girl. I got a crew of motherfuckers hustling for me, and we move serious weight–"

"I know–"

"No, listen. I do a lot of shit that will send me away forever if I ever get caught. I need to know that I can trust you and that you're strong and can deal with the bullshit that comes along with being with a man that's in the game this deep."

If I wasn't strong, I wanted to be for him...just for him. He was Clyde, and I was so ready to be Bonnie. Shit, even when reading all of those hood books, I thought that being with a street nigga was just about being fucked good, being the envy of all the other women, and being laced with diamonds and labels. But King had showed me that it was so much more than that. I was kept. I was loved. He had my back, and I was ready to have his.

"I got you, baby," I assured him.

And he smiled that adorable smile at me and leaned over and kissed my cheek. "Bet. Now let's eat."

That was four months ago, and ever since, I had been the happiest bitch in this world.

"Tesientes tan bien, Reina. Teamo."

He knew what he was doing talking that shit to me. Ain't nothing like a bilingual dope boy, I swear! His swag plus intelligence is what turned me the fuck on and made me buck on his dick as he rode me with no mercy.

"Fuck," he growled. "I'm cumming, baby."

"Then cum on," I encouraged him through heavy breathing. "You're so hard. I feel it. Cum, baby."

Our eyes connected, and it was like electricity. He sat up, held on to my waist and pounded this pussy until he was cumming. "Arrrrgh!"

Within seconds, he collapsed next to me. You could hear nothing in his house but our panting and the cold wind blowing outside.

We lay there speechless for a few minutes before he reached over and started to rub my bare, sweaty stomach. "I want you to apply to Spelman. If you get accepted, I'll pay for it."

My eyes shot toward him. "Why?"

"Because that's where you really want to go."

Anxiety filled me, so I propped myself up on my elbows. "Spelman is so far away. What about *us*?"

"I'll come see you every weekend if I have to. I'll fly you home every other weekend if I gotta." Then he shrugged his shoulders. "Hell, I can even come stay down there for a week at a time if I want to."

What he was saying may have sounded good to him, but what it sounded like to me was that he was pushing us apart just when I was the happiest I had ever been because we were together.

He saw the sadness creeping into my eyes, so he reached for me, put my body under his and spooned with me. With my back to him, he hovered over me and kissed my cheek.

"I'd never leave you, but I'm not selfish. I want you to have everything you want in life, and if Spelman is what you want, it's what you'll get."

I was reluctant, but, for the past six months, I had trusted King with all of me, so I had to trust that he really was doing this for me and not to get rid of me. I had to trust that if I got accepted, we would still be Bonnie and Clyde.

"Okay. It shouldn't be too late to apply for the next school year. I will apply tomorrow." Then I let out a small sigh, happy that my dreams were coming true both emotionally and educationally. I just hoped that both would continue to work out like I wanted them to.

He kissed me again as he told me, "I love you."

"How much?" I asked, with a girlish grin.

"More than anything."

I smiled in satisfaction as I returned the love. "I love you too."

I could feel his smile as his cheek lay on top of mine. "How much?"

I thought for a few seconds, trying to top his reply. "More than Kanye loves Kanye."

And then we broke out into uncontrollable giggles as we playfully touched each other with all the love in the world.

KING

I had fallen so hard for that pretty young thang. The shit was embarrassing, but every time that I was around her, every time that tight pussy was wrapped around my dick, I didn't give two fucks about what anybody thought.

I mean, who wouldn't wife that up? She was pretty, thick, and smart as hell. She was ambitious when most bitches' goals were limited to getting wifed by the next nigga so they wouldn't have to do shit. She had dreams and aspirations when I had never even met a chick who wanted to go to college. She had a nigga's back. She trusted me, my decisions, and anything I said. She was so driven and full of life that the shit was addictive, and it made me hustle harder.

Yeah, I had been fucked over by Tiana, and I moved on rather quickly. To be honest, I never thought I would even give a fuck about another chick again, let alone *love her*, but Kennedy brought out feelings in me that a nigga didn't even know he had. I thought that I loved Tiana, but since hooking up with Kennedy, I realized that I didn't. If I had, I wouldn't have lied to her, and I wouldn't have cheated. With Kennedy, I didn't lie. I told her *almost* everything, and I hadn't hit another bitch since climbing in that pussy. Shorty was bad, and she was mine.

"What's that corny ass look on your face, bruh?"

I looked up from my plate of jerk chicken at Dolla, who was giving me this goofy ass look. Jada had done us a favor and picked us up some food on the way to the crib. Me, Meech, and Dolla were breaking bread before discussing some business. I wanted to expand business down to the Carolinas, where my closest cousin had moved to with his baby mama. He was in the game as well, but he was finally ready to step it up. Expanding business meant cutting a few heads off of some other connects down there and ending the supply. But I had a few soldiers that thought nothing of that type of shit.

"*That* look is the look of a nigga who's pussy whipped!" Meech hollered, and then they both started to chuckle like that shit was cute.

"Man, fuck both of y'all." I just ignored them niggas as I felt my phone vibrating in my pocket. As soon as I took it out and saw that it was Siren, I hit ignore and put it back in my pocket.

Initially, Siren never blew my phone up, but ever since the wedding, she had been finding one reason or another to call me. I knew that that was my fault because I had fucked her that night. But I hadn't fucked her again since. I knew that she had to have heard that I was fucking with Kennedy now, but leave it to her not to give a fuck. That was typical.

"Nah, for real, though, bruh," Dolla told me. "Shorty cool?"

I knew what Dolla was asking. He wanted to be sure that I could trust Kennedy and that she wasn't just on some come up shit like Tiana. Kennedy was nothing of the sort. Yeah, I knew that

I had made that same mistake by assuming that about Tiana, but something about Kennedy spoke to a place in my heart that Tiana never did. After Tiana, I expected them to be suspicious of any woman that I fucked with, though.

"She's good. Shorty earned her position. She can have it," I said with a sly grin, thinking of how good Kennedy had been to me, in particularly how good that pussy was that morning,

Meech and Dolla chuckled slyly as if they knew exactly what I was referring to.

"Speaking of shorties and positions," Meech started. "What y'all think of me hooking up with Siren?"

Dolla and I froze and looked at Meech, questioning if he was serious, but he was.

"For real. She's cute, and she been down with us for a minute," Meech went on. "We were young when she first came around, so I really didn't pay her too much attention. But she's growing on a nigga."

Me and Siren's fling was so secret that I hadn't even told my boys. I intended for it to stay that way, especially now that I was with Kennedy. My sexual relationship with Siren was probably the only significant thing that I had never told Kennedy, and I didn't need Dolla pillow talking to his girl because she would most definitely run and tell her cousin. I wasn't hiding it from Kennedy; I was just in the habit of hiding it from everybody. Siren had been loyal enough to keep her mouth shut, so I was going to do the same for her.

We hadn't messed around in a while, but she still gave me a funny look every now and then. My attempt to wife Tiana had hurt her soul, so if she knew that I was now with Kennedy, it would tear her up. So, I'd been avoiding that drama as much as I could, but I knew the day was coming. But if she finally got the hood nigga of her dreams, maybe the news of me and Kennedy wouldn't hurt so bad.

"I say do it," I told Meech. "Like you said, she's a down ass bitch. If anything, you know she's loyal, and that shit is hard to come by."

Meech nodded slow and steady as if he was taking it all in.

"You might as well," Dolla replied. "She be around all the fucking time anyway."

Then we all broke out in laughter.

"A'ight," Meech stated with a sneaky grin. "I'ma take care of my business then. I just wanted my niggas' blessings since she was so close to the squad. Now let's get down to business. How are we going to take over the Carolinas?"

"Kevin says that it's three main suppliers down that way," I explained. "We can offer them a better deal than what their current connect is offering. Bricks are going for about twenty-eight racks down there. That's already damn near ten more than what we sell them for up this way. We can offer them twenty-four, hell, maybe even twenty-three, and still come out on top. They can either take our offer or..."

"We take them niggas out," Dolla said, finishing my sentence.

"Exactly," I agreed with a nod. "Which would start a war that we don't have enough ammunition down there to fight."

"True," Dolla nodded. "We've been operating with little bloodshed, and I'd like for it to remain that way so that my ass can stay out of jail or the ground."

"Real shit," Meech agreed. "I like being on this side of the walls and dirt, getting this money and turning up."

"So we talk to Gustavo about increasing our supply at a cheaper rate so that we can offer better prices to the suppliers in the Carolinas but still get money," I decided.

Dolla asked, "You think he'll do it?"

"We've been one of his main supplier for the west coast for about a year now," I answered. "We've done good business with him. I don't see why not."

"Cool," Meech responded with a nod as he grabbed his glass of vodka and raised it. "Then let's get this money."

Dolla and I grabbed our glasses as well, and we joined in a toast as we said in unison, "Let's get this money."

Finally, life was back on the up and up. I had a badass chick in my corner, and now I was about to expand my business.

Life couldn't have been better.

FEBRUARY 2011

CHAPTER TEN

KENNEDY

"Fuck!" I snapped as King turned onto my mother's block.

His eyes shot toward my frightened ones, but he was forced to focus back on the road. "What's wrong?"

"My daddy is here." Fear ran through my body. Suddenly, I was thirteen years old all over again and scared of what my father would do because he caught me talking to a boy. Although I had a lot more freedom now that I was staying with my mother, I still had to hide it from my father. He held the purse strings. My mother couldn't afford to pay my tuition, buy my books, or keep money in my bank account. She had changed her life and started working, but she still couldn't afford the extra mouth to feed. So my father was giving her money too. We didn't need him to know that my mother was allowing me to party and even stay the night out.

Suddenly, I wished that I would have called first so that I could have asked Jada to drop me off instead.

"It's cool, ma," King tried to assure me, but I wasn't convinced. I knew that King could have taken care of me, and he had kinda started doing that anyway. But although I trusted him, I had only known him for a few months, when my father was steady in my life. More importantly than needing my father's money, I loved him. I saw him hurt over my mother's betrayal and how her life suffered because of it. I didn't want to make him repeat that pain because of me.

But so much for that, because as King pulled in front of my mother's house, my father was standing on the porch, visibly arguing with my mother.

"Shit," I sighed.

I had told King all about how overprotective my father was, so he looked toward the house sympathetically.

"I'll call you later," I told him as I grabbed the door handle.

"Nah, I'll wait right here."

My eyes bucked. "No, King–"

When he looked me in my eyes and reiterated, "*I'll wait here*," I knew better than to argue with him.

It's too many bossy men in my life, I thought as I reluctantly left the car.

However, there was only *one* too many bossy men in my life. King's possession I could deal with because his decisions were not just best for *him*. They did not just make *him* happy. They were what was best for *me* too. He ensured my happiness always, but my father didn't give a fuck whether I was happy or not, as long as I was obeying his orders.

"Kennedy, where the hell have you been?" my father barked as soon as he saw me walking toward the house. "And who is that you're riding with?"

My father was yelling like a fucking slave master, and it was so embarrassing. As I ascended the steps, my mother looked at me with sympathy. "I told you, she spent the night at Jada's house, Ricky," she answered for me.

"Richard," he corrected my mother.

Bougie ass, I thought.

"And I told you not to let her stay out all night," my father continued fussing. "It's a weekday. She has school tomorrow. She can't keep up with her studies if she's out all night in the gawd damn streets."

As I finally made it up on the porch, I saw anger fill my mother's eyes. "You don't tell me what to do, *Richard*! You don't run my house! I pay the bills here!"

"But I give you money to support Kennedy every month and that is what I expect you to do: support her! Not let her turn into you!"

"Daddy!" I shouted in warning.

"And you!" he said, pointing his finger in my face.

I wasn't having it. I was not about to let him embarrass me in front of King, who was still parked at the curb looking on. So, I stepped by him to go into the house, but he grabbed my arm and snatched me back.

"Daddy!" I shrieked.

And my mother shouted, "Ricky, let her go!"

Just as I snatched away, and my mother grabbed me, I heard a car door slam. I could see King coming our way, and my heart beat inside of my chest uncontrollably. I was scared, not knowing what he would do or if he would hurt my father. I feared that the drama would turn him off of me completely.

But my parents just kept fussing. They didn't even notice him coming.

"You're going too far!" my mother yelled. "It's not that serious! You're too hard on her!"

"And you're too loose!" my father replied with venom in his voice. "As always."

That hurt my mother. I could tell. Her grip on my arm weakened, and so did her stance. But before she could reply, they both noticed King standing at the bottom of the steps.

His eyes were on me, but before he spoke, he quickly looked at my mother and greeted her politely, "Hi." Then he turned back to me, saying, "Let's go."

"Who the hell are you?" my father spat, looking at King's bejeweled, Pele jacket and Timberlands like they disgusted him.

As always, King's demeanor was cool, and his swagger was unfazed. "I'm Damion Carter, but you may call me King... or you can call me the man that's gon' beat the shit out of you if you put your hands on my woman again. Either one works for me, *sir*."

My mother had the most satisfied smirk on her face. She had never met King, but I had told her a lot about him. Although my father talked major shit to me and my mother, he knew better than to talk that shit to King. He saw the threat all over King and didn't want any parts of it. He just stood there grimacing; his facial expressions saying words that he knew better than to allow leave his throat.

"C'mon, Kennedy," King insisted with his hand outstretched.

My mother gave me a nod, telling me that it was okay to go to King. My father's eyes about fell out of their sockets as I walked by. I guess he was about to say something because I then heard my mother say, "Leave her alone. She's grown, Ricky. Let her be."

And then he said, "Yeah, well, let's see how far that gets her."

My heart broke as I walked down the steps. I hated to disappoint my father, but as I locked eyes with King, I knew that, if my father never spoke to me again, there was another man in my life that would take care of me forever.

As I reached the bottom of the stairs, King took my hand, and before we could walk away from the house, he turned to my mother. "Ma'am, it was nice meeting you."

And she smiled bashfully. His demeanor had the same effect on her as it had on any other woman that crossed his path. "You too, sweetie."

I heard my father suck his teeth as I walked with King to the car hand–in–hand. I was shocked to see how easy it was to stand up to my father, but I was sure that it was only because King was there. I knew that I would feel the repercussions later.

King opened my door and guided me in. After he shut it, I glanced up at my mother's house. She was smiling at the car while my father walked down the steps, shaking his head in disappointment.

Once King climbed into the driver's seat, I sighed. "My dad is going to freak. I guess I can kiss school goodbye."

King looked at me like I was crazy. "If I'm willing to pay for you to go to Spelman, you don't think I'll pay your tuition here?"

I was dumbstruck.

"Baby, being your man don't mean that I just get the pussy when I want to. I know I've just bought you little things, and I've given you money here and there, but that's because, unlike the other chicks that I've dated, you don't need for shit. But if that's because your father is doing it, don't worry. Now, *Daddy's* got you."

Despite my anxiety, lust swam through my body as King gently grabbed my chin and kissed my lips. Again, I trusted him, so as he turned the engine, I had absolutely no worries.

KING

"Shit," I mumbled as I glanced at the Caller ID.

I didn't feel like her shit, especially on top of the day that I'd had already. I had experienced enough drama for the day. I was chilling in my living room, trying to calm down with a couple of shots of Remy while Kennedy showered for dinner.

I was about ready to kill that old man, but that was when I realized how much I loved that girl. I usually would have put that nigga's face to the pavement without thinking twice. But I knew how much Kennedy loved her pops, despite how overprotective he was. I cared about her more than my need to do damage, which shocked the shit out of me.

Despite my irritation, I answered the phone. "What up, Siren?"

"Hey, King. What you doin'?"

"Waiting on Kennedy to get out of the shower so that we can head to the restaurant. What's good? Something going on that I need to know about that Meech or Dolla couldn't tell me?"

That was a clue for her to say what the hell she had to say and get off of the phone, but she only sucked her teeth and huffed. Yet, I remained silent, waiting for her to get on with it. Back in the day when it was only me, Meech, and Dolla running shit, Jada and Siren would make runs for us. They were two young girls in a car that the police would never suspect or search if stopped while on the e-way. Even now, they made large deliveries for us because they were the only ones that we could trust to get it done. So, the only calls she should have been making to me at the moment should have been about business.

But knowing Siren, I knew better, so prepared myself.

Instantly, I heard irritation as Siren blew out a breath. "In the *shower*? She living with you now?"

"If she is, what's it to you?"

"A lot!" she shrieked with hurt in her voice. "Is that why you haven't been fucking with me?"

Fuck it. She might as well know. "Yeah."

"That little girl means that much to you that you're through fucking with me after all these years?"

"She's my woman, Siren." I felt like that was enough for her to understand why I wasn't fucking with her, but apparently it wasn't.

"And? That's never stopped you before. A girlfriend has never stopped you from getting this pussy. Hell, a fiancée didn't either–"

"Kennedy is different."

More hurt fell from her throat. "*Different*?"

"Yeah. What's your point in all of this, Siren?"

"I miss you," she moaned, and I rolled my eyes to the back of my head.

"How? It's been a long ass time since we smashed."

"I was giving you space. I knew that what Tiana did fucked you up. I thought you was just chillin', not over there falling in love with the next bitch–"

"Watch your mouth." When she fell silent in my threat, I continued to check her jealous ass. "You knew I was fucking with her."

"Yes, *fucking* with her, not *wifing* her." It sounded like it slit her throat to say the words. The realization cut like a knife. I knew it.

She took a deep breath and changed her tone. "King, I miss you."

I was sure that she did. For a long time, I had been constant dick in her life. And I was sure that, to her, I was more than dick. We hung out and vibed as friends, but fucked liked lovers at night. But I never gave her any inclination that we were more than fuck buddies. It wasn't my fault that she'd been obliviously living in a fairytale.

Luckily, I was saved by the bell. The doorbell rang, and that was my cue to hang up. "I gotta go, Siren."

"King–"

"I'll holla at you later." I hung up before she could beg anymore. I had very little sympathy for Siren. She didn't miss me. She missed being the jump off of a dope boy. She missed her position and status, even if nobody knew about it but us.

Hopefully, Meech was working his way on giving her what she needed so desperately.

Now who the fuck is this? Nobody ever came to my crib unannounced. Shit, nobody even knew where I stayed but Meech, Dolla, and a few of the employees that worked right up under us. But when I looked through the peephole, I remembered.

What the fuck is this bitch doing here? I ran my hands over my head as she rang the bell again. *Ain't this a bitch?*

When she started holding down the doorbell, I hurried and flung the door open. "What the fuck do you want?"

Tiana's eyes bucked at my hostility, but when I didn't budge, her expression softened. "Hi. How are you?"

I looked at that bitch like she was crazy. I hadn't seen her since the day of our wedding. And since then she obviously had fed off. I loved a thick woman, so she was thick too, but she had gained a few pounds, and it was obvious as hell. The last few times that I'd seen her, she was draped in all of the nice clothes and jewelry that I had given her over the years, but now she had obviously been forced to go back to Target and Forever 21.

Although she blew my phone up after I walked out of the wedding, I ignored that bitch and kept it pushing. I had heard through the streets that that nigga, Money, still played her. He never wifed her ass, and now she was living on the East Side with her mama.

"I'm good. What's the deal?"

She tried to hide how my dry reaction to her presence hurt her. She forced a smile as she ran her hand through a bad weave. "Can I come in?"

I couldn't even control how ugly of a look I gave her. "Man, *hell* nah. What the fuck do you want?"

She was so hurt that I saw her chest fall from the weight of the blow to her ego. "It's like that, King? After all that we had, you can't even talk to me?'

"All that we had?" Now, I was looking at her like she was straight up belligerent. "Did you give a fuck about what we had while you was running up after that nigga, Money?"

She lowered eyes shamefully and stared at the ground.

"Get the fuck away from crib, Tiana."

"King, I miss you."

What the fuck? Is it "I miss King day" today or some shit?

I sneered as I ran my hand over my head in frustration. As I gave Tiana the look of death, I noticed her staring behind me with a surprised look on her face. Before I could turn around, two soft arms wrapped around my waist. Kennedy's hot pink nails popped off of my white tee as she traced my body. Since one of my hands was on the doorknob, and the other was resting on the frame of the doorway, Kennedy was able to stick her head out under my arm as she held me from behind.

"Hey, baby." She spoke so softly and sincere, as if Tiana wasn't even standing right there. "I'm ready for dinner. How do I look?"

I tried to hold back my amused smirk, but I couldn't. *Damn, my baby is a G.* I turned my head slightly to look down at her. "You look beautiful, baby. This is Tiana."

"Oh. I didn't know that we had company, babe." Now, she was putting on the extra polite voice. She sounded like a damn customer service rep. The shit was hilarious. Then she smiled at Tiana. "Nice to meet you."

I didn't know if Tiana still felt like she had rights to me, so something would pop off, or if Kennedy would slap this bitch. I wasn't worried either way. I wouldn't let Tiana say two harsh words to Kennedy, and if my baby wanted to throw them hands, I would let her.

But, being my queen, Kennedy simply stood on her tip toes and kissed my lips slowly. "I'll be waiting in the living room. Love you."

"Love you too, baby."

Tiana could have died! And I wanted to laugh in her fucking face, but, shit, Kennedy had played it so cool that I had to follow her lead.

As she walked away from the door, I looked at Tiana, ignoring how sick to her stomach she looked. "I gotta go. Have a nice night."

And before she could say anything, I closed the door.

Damn, what a day.

SIREN

Waiting for Kennedy to get out of the shower so that we can head to the restaurant. King's words rang through my mind like a broken record. *She's different.* I lay on my bed crying tears that would overflow Lake Michigan.

"He did it to me again," I sobbed. But I blamed myself. For years, I had committed myself to a man that had never even spoken a word of wanting me in that way. I loved him when he didn't ask me to. I honestly expected for my heart to break in unfixable pieces one day. Today was that day, and even though I had expected it, I still was not prepared for how truly bad it hurt.

Luckily, when my phone rang, I was forced to sit up and dry my tears. It was Meech, so I knew that it was about business. King had always been in the background since he was the boss. He, Meech, and Dolla were partners, but Dolla and Meech did most of the footwork that was necessary. They organized the drops that Jada and I made, collected money, and what not. It was King's money from hustling in his teens that made the first purchase of weight that spearheaded this organization a few years ago, so he mostly stayed back in the cut, only surfacing when necessary. But he had *really* fallen back since he started fucking with Kennedy. Yet, I was starting to realize that maybe he had just fallen back from me.

"Hello?"

"Siren? You okay?"

I continued wiping my face as I forced some happiness into my voice as I responded, "Yeah, I'm good, Meech. What's going on? You need me to do something?"

"Yeah," came out in a slow, cautious tone that I had never heard him use before. "I need you to come hang out with me tonight."

"I don't really feel like driving to the spot. Let me see if Jada feels like picking me–"

"No, no, no," he interrupted. "All of us won't be hanging out...just *me* and *you*."

"Huh?"

When he chuckled, a little of my hurt went away because I could feel the lust and flirtation through the phone. I was still shocked, though. Meech had playfully made a few comments here and there about my body and hinted that I was cute. But he had never ever outright flirted with me.

"You heard me, girl."

I giggled. "Stop playing with me, Meech."

"I'm serious, ma. I wanna fuck with you."

"Fuck with me, huh?" I teased. "Quit playing, Meech. Are you over there getting high with Dolla or something? This ain't funny, and I ain't in the mood for y'all to be cracking jokes about this later."

I could just hear it now, and the thought made me cringe, imagining them roasting me while King looked on like the shit was funny.

"I'm serious as a heart attack." Meech's voice came through the phone in a genuine baritone that made me shiver, though I had yet to take him seriously. "And ain't nobody gotta know about this if you don't want them to."

I looked at myself in the mirror. Confusion was all over my face. "Where is all of this coming from?" I asked Meech.

"It's been on my mind for a minute, I can't lie. You're always around with that phat ol' ass. What do you expect?" I giggled as he continued, "Nah, for real. I mean, when we first met, I never looked at you like that. I respected the fact that you was Jada's best friend. I didn't want to fuck with one of her friends on no bullshit. But a nigga's grown now. I know what I want, and I want *you*."

A lustful grin spread across my face. I had had my nose in King's ass for years, but I never denied how fine Meech was. He had locs like King's, but his were shorter because he had just started growing them two years ago. He was an even six feet, and for my 5'3" frame, he was tall like I liked them. He was thick too. He and King lifted weights together all the time, so he was just as cocky as King, but his muscles were covered with a light vanilla coating, versus King's dark coffee skin tone. He didn't have as much money as King either, but, as his right-hand man, his bank account would equal King's in no time.

"Sure," I finally answered him. "I'll come kick it with you."

He wasn't King, but he would do for the night. And hell, King was fucking my friend, so I might as well fuck his.

Present day

Two days after release

CHAPTER ELEVEN

KENNEDY

Since my mother was too old to be in some club partying, she made her own little celebration at her house. She still stayed in the same house on the south side that she had back then. As I slowly walked into the house, I saw that absolutely nothing had changed in three years. Pictures of me, from all ages, were still all over the wall. That ugly ass picture of me at junior prom, wearing a dress way too big because my father refused to allow me to wear something clingy, was still the biggest picture on the wall. My date, Carl, the lead saxophonist in the band at the time, with huge crater-like pimples on his face and coke-bottle glasses still made me cringe when I looked at him, holding me like that moment was the closest he would ever get to a girl in his life.

"Oooh!" My mama squealed at a high-pitch, hugged me and held onto me for dear life right there in the hallway. I held her tight, and as I did, it felt like time had stood still. For seconds, I just enjoyed the feeling of her cheek against mine and her scent in my nose.

"I missed you so much," I cried.

"I missed you too, baby."

We were so busy crying and rocking that we didn't notice Kayla, who wanted my mother's undivided attention.

"Grandma! Grandma!" She even had the nerve to suck her teeth. "Hi, Grandma, dang!"

I have really got to teach this lil' girl how to watch her damn mouth.

"Kayla!" King warned her as he held her in his arms, standing close behind me.

"Oh, leave my grandbaby alone!" my mother said in a weird baby voice.

"That's what's wrong with her now," King told her.

"Oh hush." My mother waved her hand dismissively as she took Kayla from him. She straddled her on her hip and then took me by the hand. "Both of my babies are here! I can't believe it! Come on in! I got some food waiting for you."

Even though I wasn't looking forward to seeing my father, I was expecting to see him. Last night, I told my mother to go ahead and invite him over so that I could kill two birds with one stone, but as we left the hall and entered the living room, I saw that it was empty. King's eyes found mine and they were full of empathy and compassion, but I didn't need it. My father hadn't found anything important enough to set aside his anger in order to be there for me, not even the birth of Kayla or my incarceration, so his absence today wasn't a total shocker. However, it was noticeable, and it created a weird tension that my mother attempted to talk over.

"C'mon on. Don't you worry," she told me, still leading me through the house by the hand. "I got this hot food ready for y'all. We gon' sit down and eat like a family, because *we* are family. Ain't nobody missing from this table, chil'."

My mother and father were still at odds. Actually, my sentencing had made their estranged relationship worse. During our phone calls over the last three years, my mother would tell me how she would call my father, furious that he was still so stubborn that he wouldn't even be there for me during my time of need. During those arguments, he had blamed her for my imprisonment. I wanted to be like her, he said. I had taken after her hood fantasies, he said.

But I can't lie, as we sat at that table surrounded by fried chicken, baked macaroni and cheese, dressing, and every other signature soul food dish that a prisoner imagines scarfing down the moment that they step outside of that gate, we did look the typical ghetto family; the young grandmother that hadn't raised her daughter, the toddler with the flippant mouth, the dope dealer, and the felon. Oddly, at this table, however, the dope dealer wasn't the only felon at the table.

Despite it all, I hadn't felt that much love since before I went to prison, and I would do time all over again if it meant that I could preserve the existence of this happiness forever.

****

"I want to go back to school, King."

King glanced at me quickly as we rode the expressway toward our home. Dinner was great. I had been home for three days, and I had slept with my man, kissed my smart-mouthed daughter, and hugged my friends. But now that I had sat with my mother, the only other person in this world besides King that had unconditionally loved me, I felt like I was officially back home with my family.

"Why?"

"Why not?" I asked with a shrug.

"You just got home. You don't want to chill for a while?"

I chuckled sarcastically as I stared out of the window. "I've chilled for three years, King. I want to live."

As if he realized what he had said, he slid his hand onto the sensitive, inner area of my exposed thigh. Instantly, as the passionate lover that my man is came to the surface, the small irritation that I thought I was about to feel was diffused just as quickly as it was created.

"I'm sorry," he told me in his rough, seductive voice. "You're right."

"School has always been a big part of my life, baby," I insisted. "Besides you and Kayla, it was my passion. I want to finish what I started."

There were rare moments when I saw anxiety in King's eyes, and this was one of them. He looked worried as he asked, "At Spelman?"

I instantly soothed him by returning his loving gesture; I put my hand on his thigh and squeezed, our arms now crossed over the other. "No, I would never leave you and Kayla again, even though she can't stand me." We both broke out in quiet uncontrollable giggles since Kayla was sleeping soundly in the backseat.

"I just..." I sighed, the assurance in my heart confirming my decision. "I just want to be the girl that I was before...before...you know. I want to be Kennedy, not this girl that just got out of prison. I was passionate about child psychology, and I want to get my degree. I don't know if a felon would ever get hired at a practice, or even be able to get licensed, for that matter, but I at least want my degree."

King smiled and quickly leaned over and kissed me as the light changed. "Okay, baby. You can do whatever you want. And don't worry about whether you'll get hired or not. You get your degree and license and then you can start your own private practice. How about that?"

I was beaming. "Really?"

"Yeah, really."

Still smiling, I rested my head against the headrest, imagining myself in my pencil skirt and blazer, counseling children with ADHD, autism, and Asperger's Syndrome. It wasn't the hood dreams that I'd had when I was younger, but it was definitely a dream that I wished would come true.

King

After dinner, I met up with Dolla and Meech at a lounge on the South Side. A drink was definitely needed. I had enjoyed a great dinner with my family. Finally, things were feeling back to normal...all except the sudden appearance of the police who were investigating Terry's murder.

Since Dolla had been questioned the other day, we had spotted undercover cars outside of our homes. The shit was no coincidence. The police hadn't suddenly come across some new and telling evidence from a five-year-old murder. Somebody had snitched. That was a sickening feeling since only the three of us knew about it. But we knew better than to ever assume that it was one of us three that had spoken to the police. If one of us went down, we all did. Although I had initially financed this game, our supplier had gotten used to working with all three of us; so had many of the niggas that copped weight from us. If one of us went down, there would be so much suspicion around us that no one would work with any of us.

But it looked like we were about to figure out who the leak was. Meech had called us to a local bar, Raven's Place, because he felt like he had figured out who it was.

"It's that stupid ass nigga, Lock."

Lock was this local nigga that got rid of the van for us. He didn't know what we had used it for, but its description was all over the news the actual day of, and the days following, Terry's murder. Looking back on it, it was probably dumb as fuck for us to leave that dump in his hands, but he was a pro at the shit. He wasn't a dealer; his hustle was stealing cars, getting money for the valuable parts and torching the rest of it.

"I heard the nigga got arrested two weeks ago. He got caught in a stolen car, but the nigga got out with no charge." Meech spoke with so much excitement, like he was so relieved that he'd figured this shit out. "Dolla was the one that dropped the van off to him, which is probably why the police are connecting the shit to him. Lock had to have snitched, man."

We all sat at the bar in silence for a few seconds, thinking. In my mind, Meech was right. That was the only logical explanation. We had been clean, meticulous even. There was no way that the police should've been sniffing around our back doors unless someone had given them a reason to. And it wasn't one of us, so it had to be Lock.

I really didn't want this type of heat around, especially with Kennedy just getting home. This shit had to be dealt with quick. Since it didn't seem like the cops had any more evidence than Dolla being linked to this van, we had to dead the situation before it got any worse.

"Well," I said with a grimace. "Let's do what we gotta do then."

Present day

Three days after release

CHAPTER TWELVE

KENNEDY

♪But I'm promisin' you better though
And your friends sayin' let him go
And we ain't gettin' any younger
I can give up now but I can promise you forever though
If there's a question of my heart, you've got it. It don't belong to
anyone but you♪

I laughed to myself as I followed King's horrendous singing. *"'If there's a question of my love, you've got it. Baby, don't worry, I've got plans for you.'"*

The sound of nails on a chalkboard led me into the kitchen, where King was in front of the stove, wearing nothing but boxers as he fried, what smelled like, bacon.

Despite King's fucked up singing, I leaned against the doorway and listened. I loved the song. When it was released back in March, I would lie in my cell and listen to it on repeat, thinking of me, King, and our wedding. Although that day was surrounded by so much chaos, it was still so loving and ghetto... just like us.

As if he felt my presence, he turned and caught me leaning in the doorway with my nose turned up at his impression of Usher. He didn't say a word. He just cracked that signature smile and reached his arms out to me, summoning me toward that dreadful voice, as he swayed to the beat of *Matrimony*. Despite the headache resulting from his high, off pitch tone, I went to him anyway, drawn toward his sexual darkness like a zombie.

"*'Baby, I've been making plans. Making plans! Oh, love! Aw, ba-bae!'*" I cringed while he sang as I took his hands. Despite my obvious discomfort, he pulled me in, under him and began to sway back and forth to Usher and Wale. "*'Baby, I've been making plans for you. Yeah. Making plans! Aw ba-bae! Baby, I've been making plans...'*"

I was giggling uncontrollably, but I kept dancing. No matter how strenuous the discomfort was in my ears, I had been waiting to be in his arms again for way too long to give a fuck about him sounding like a cat dying on my ear drum. Luckily for my ears, the bacon started to pop in its grease, so he had to let me go.

"You're in a good mood," I said with a smile. I was teasing him, but I was happy to see it. Whatever had encouraged his sudden flight out of the house yesterday had formed a grey cloud over his usual happy demeanor. It had also put a cloud over my homecoming. But just as fast as it formed above, it appeared to be gone.

He looked back over his shoulder. "I am," he agreed with a smile.

I hopped up on a stool that was in front of the island. "What's the special occasion?"

"Just took care of some shit that's been hindering business a little bit."

Knowing that he wouldn't go into detail, my eyebrow still kissed my forehead in suspicion. "Took care of it?"

"Well, it *will be* taken care of later." And as if to take my mind off of the bullshit, he turned and asked, "Want some coffee? You used to love this shit while you were in school."

And I went on ahead and let him change the subject. "Yes, I do. Speaking of school, I'm going to go up to the school today to see about enrolling for this upcoming semester."

Standing at the Keurig machine, he lovingly smiled at me. "Good. I'm proud of you."

I looked on in fascination as he prepared the Keurig machine to brew. King had hit it on the head when he said that I loved coffee. Every college student did. Soon after I was locked up, on a visit, King had told me how he'd gotten this fancy ass machine just for me. I was still used to an old-fashioned coffee pot, but in the time that I was away, so much had changed. However minor, the smallest things, like the evolution of a single brew coffee pot, was amazing to me.

I was staring so intently at the machine that I didn't even notice that King had left it until he was standing in front of me. The remnants of the Tom Ford cologne from last night still lingered on his skin, and it sent shock waves through my body, coupled with delightful memories of the sex that had put me into a sound sleep.

"Somebody's birthday is coming up."

I smiled and instantly felt the sting of tears. "I know." After spending my last three birthdays away from my family in a cell, with women who had become family singing a very sad version of the birthday song, I was so grateful that I'd be spending my next one with him.

King approached me with the most mischievous grin. As I blushed, I couldn't help but stare at his curly afro top. "You miss my locs?" he asked, as he rubbed his hand over his cut.

"I missed *you*. I don't care what your hair looks like. You could have a fucking nappy, untamed afro for all I give a damn."

King chuckled as he wrapped his arms around my waist. I leaned into his chest and basked in his scent and touch.

"Sooo... Guess what we're doing for your birthday."

I smiled against his chest, asking, "What?"

"I never got to take you on that honeymoon, so we're going."

My smile was almost embarrassing. I knew I looked like the naïve kid he'd met five years ago. "Really?!"

He looked down at my face, his face giving me all of the life that I needed. "Yes, really. We're going to Cabo, baby."

****

The counselor immediately looked threatened as me, Jada and Siren walked into the small office. Despite the fact that we were all dressed in clothes that cost more than her monthly salary, she looked at the three, black women sitting across from her prestigious white face like we were trouble makers.

"May I help you?" She sat on the other side of the desk, elderly, pink and wrinkled with judgment all over her face. I was sure that we looked like the wives on the reality shows that her grandchildren watched on television.

"You may," I returned. "I'm interested in enrolling for next semester, but there is a bit of an issue."

"Issue?" she questioned with a glare. "What's your student ID number?"

"I don't recall."

She attempted to grimace discreetly, but I caught it. "First and last name?"

Jada and Siren had already had it with her presumptuous attitude, but my eyes asked them to chill as I replied, "Kennedy Desiree Carter."

"Date of birth?"

"June 5, 1992."

She made a few key strokes and was oddly quiet for quite a few minutes. In fact, she was so quiet that the three of us sat uncomfortably, beginning to fume at this bitch's discourtesy.

"I see," she finally spit. "You dropped out."

"I didn't drop out."

"Well, you were enrolled and–"

"I was arrested." Her eyes widened and then narrowed, as if whatever preconceived notions she had formed when we walked in were now confirmed. But I went on, further confirming them. "I served three years. I was released a few days ago, and I would like to continue with my program. Is that possible since I am a convicted felon?"

She looked me up and down and then glanced back at the screen. I knew what she was looking at. She was checking out my grades. As she stared, her demeanor softened, and her defense weakened. It was as if she was looking at the good grades and the 3.8 GPA, wondering how in the hell had I ended up in prison.

"What were you convicted for?"

I knew she had asked that question out of pure nosiness alone. It had nothing to do with what I needed to know, yet I responded anyway. "Drug trafficking."

There was more awkward silence that accompanied her silent questions. Jada and Siren shifted uncomfortably in their seats. I knew that they were ready to tell the old lady off, but my cool demeanor was directing them to take it easy on the old broad.

Finally, she sighed, saying, "The problem is not if you will be able to enroll, the problem is *financial aid*. As a convicted felon, you're not eligible for many funding sources–"

Before I could even stop her, Jada interrupted her. "Are you talking about money?" Then she laughed. "That's not an issue. *Next.*"

She cleared her throat as she tore her eyes away from Jada. "I see that you were a psychology major. State licensing boards typically require a minimum of a doctoral degree in psychology from a regionally accredited or government-chartered institution. Most doctoral programs are very competitive to get into with minimum slots available. Even if you maintain these impeccable grades, department heads may prefer to give those minimal slots to someone who doesn't have a criminal background such as yours."

"Say I get into a doctoral program, then what?" I pressed.

"The Department of Financial and Professional Regulation may refuse to issue a license if you've been convicted of a felony." She saw my disappointment and went in for the kill. "Depending upon the nature of the crime and the age you were when convicted, you will eventually be eligible to have the charge expunged from your record through a gubernatorial pardon. They're *not* easy to come by, and they take a number of *years* to obtain in order to prove that you're reformed. You sound like the type of person that might definitely benefit from one, though. In the meantime, I suggest you find a career path in which you can work with a background like yours, that...you know...that have been to prison."

"This bitch," Siren muttered, her leg bouncing repeatedly with frustration.

The old lady's eyes darted at Siren, but before the obscenity brewing in her mind could vomit out of her mouth, Jada, once again, spoke up, "But you said 'may'."

The old lady looked at her oddly. "Excuse me?"

"You said most department heads *may* choose to give those slots to someone else," she explained as she gathered her purse. "And you said that the Department of Financial and Professional Regulation *may* refuse to issue her a license. That means she still has a chance."

She was right, and I was reassured. Siren and I both smiled with relief as the old lady once again failed to be discreet with her grimace.

"C'mon girl," Jada insisted to me as she stood. "Let's go register you for classes."

KING

"I didn't say shit! I swear!"

Dolla swung and shut Lock up with one agonizing punch to the jaw.

"Aarrrgh!" Lock squirmed on the cold concrete floor of the warehouse, only wearing the Sean John boxer briefs that he was wearing when we tore him out of bed a few hours ago.

"Man, I'm tired of hearing this nigga cry," Dolla snapped. "Can we dead that ass or what?"

Dolla, Meech, and even Lock looked on as they waited on my demands, but Lock's eyes were full of requests for mercy.

"What you waitin' on?" I asked Dolla. "End this shit."

I watched as Lock lay on the ground staring into the barrel of Dolla's pistol. Although a young twenty-five-year-old, he had decided to stop the whining and face his death like a man, making him a bigger man than I. He wasn't a part of my crew, but I had watched the little nigga grow up in my hood. Despite others that we'd murked, he was cool with us; a friend. I thought of him as one of the youngins that I'd help mature into a real hustler. So before Dolla could pull the trigger, I was turning my back, on my way out of the warehouse.

I heard him fire off two shots before I heard Meech ask, "Should we call the cleanup crew or do this shit ourselves?"

I shot over my shoulder, "Do it yourselves."

"Man, I'm wearing Ferragamo," Meech complained as he sucked his teeth. "I can't get blood on Ferragamo, fam."

I turned to face them, the sight of Lock's head leaking dark blood filling my eyesight. "Really? The fuck? Are you a fashionista or some shit?" I asked Meech, with a smirk. "You sound like a bitch."

"Easy for you to say while you're walking out this motherfucka. Where you goin'?'

"I got some other pressin' matters to attend to. You know that."

"True, true," he nodded. "Go handle your business then, bruh. Catch up later."

"Bet. I'll holla at y'all."

They both replied, "One," and then I could hear the chainsaw being cranked.

MEECH

After four days of chaos, the dust had finally settled. Kennedy was adjusting, and we had silenced the police's snitch. Finally, everything was back like it once was; it was all good in the hood.

Well, I wasn't exactly in the hood. I let out a sigh of relief as I turned into my circle driveway, I looked at my five-thousand square feet of house and land and was grateful. I spotted Elijah peeking out of his bedroom window, as he always did at night when he heard the garage door opening, and I was even more grateful.

Once again, I had spared my family the hurt and pain of losing everything they had, specifically the hurt and pain of losing me.

As I stepped out of my "work car," a 2015 Lexus LX truck, I was thankful for every little thing: The work car, the four car garage, and the multiple luxury vehicles that were surrounding me, including my baby–a slick ass, cherry red Ferrari. I left the garage and entered my house that some would consider a small mansion. I was appreciative of the foyer, the marble flooring, and the crystal chandeliers. For the last few days, I had been faced with the threat of losing all of this. That threat had me so much more appreciate of every little thing.

Facing a murder charge would have killed me. I was a G, so could serve time like a man, but knowing that being away from my family would hurt them, would undoubtedly be the death of me. I had watched King suffer that same emotional death for the past three years. He hadn't gone to jail, but it had been way worse than that; his girl had. Living with that guilt had killed him, and I never wanted to trade places with him. That's why I was more than happy to do what I had to do tonight at the warehouse.

As I walked into the kitchen, I was even more thankful. Standing at the stove, cooking, what smelled like, my favorite meal was *my woman.* She ended up my woman by chance. One day she walked into the spot, and I just saw her in a different light. It was like I had matured suddenly. All of her years of devotion to my squad had made her that much more beautiful in my eyes, and I was intent on making her my woman. It wasn't as hard as I'd thought it would be. I called her, I asked her out and we spent that night and every night since together. Just like she had been for my crew, she was ride or die for me. In return, I was the father to her son that he'd never had. Now, four years later, we were a power couple in my eyes. She was the Bonnie to my Clyde, still willing to ride for the squad, count money, weigh dope, and make whatever move that I needed.

"Mmm," she moaned seductively, as I wrapped my hands around her waist, her big ass grazing against my dick and causing it to jump. "Hey you."

"Hey yourself. How was your day?"

"Good. Elijah and I watched as they set up his playground in the backyard. That shit took all afternoon. Thanks for buying it for him, by the way."

"You don't have to thank me. That's my son, and he said he was tired of walking to the park, so I put the park in the backyard."

I could see the appreciation all over Siren's face. It was all in her eyes, but she knew better than to say anything else. Elijah was my son and, like her, I would do anything for him. "How was your day?"

"It was cool." I shrugged. "Nothing major." Yeah, I was wrong for lying, but, like King, I wanted to keep my family as far away from the bullshit as possible. That meant lying a little and leaving out the really bad things that we had to do sometimes to keep our families together.

She knew that I was lying too. It was like she felt it, but she knew how I felt. Everything wasn't her business, and Lock's murder, or anyone else's for that matter, was not her business.

"Well," she said bringing back her smile. "I'm glad you made it home early tonight. I'm almost done cooking. It's your favorite."

"I see," I said into her neck as I kissed it.

"Here, taste it." She dipped her spoon in the homemade pesto sauce and held it to my mouth.

I licked the spoon, and, as always, it was just right. "That shit is on point. I can't wait to eat it...and eat *you* later."

She grinned and smacked my shoulder, which felt like nothing because, though curvy, she was short with small feet and hands. "You so nasty."

Just as I kissed her and was about to say something even nastier, Elijah came charging into the kitchen.

"Dad!" he yelled as he ran to me and wrapped his arms around my legs.

I playfully nudged him. "What's up, Lil' Man?"

"I've been waiting for you all day so that we can play the game!"

"A'ight. We can go play while your mama finishes cookin'. I'm the Lakers, though."

He sucked his teeth. "No! I want to be the Lakers!"

"Well, how about this? First one to make it upstairs, wins. Deal?"

And before he could even agree, I took off running, and he screamed, trying to follow me.

"Be careful, Elijah!" Siren shouted, but there was no need for her concern. I was only jogging because I was going to let him win. They were my family, so I would always sacrifice to let them win.

September 2011

Chapter Thirteen

Kennedy

The day after King confronted my father, I called the old man. I knew that he was angry, and I honestly didn't know what I could say to make it right.

I was relieved when he didn't answer. But after a week of ignored calls, it hurt more than anything. Then he stopped paying my tuition, and I was as heartbroken as I was on the day that I saw Reese fucking my best friend. . Luckily, King did as promised and started paying my tuition. He had even bought me a white Audi a few months ago. Still, I missed the man that raised me, but fortunately, God had given me a replacement.

Once I felt like I was fully free from my father's watchful eye, I started spending more and more time in King's home, until I just never went back to my mother's house, except to pack my clothes.

King's home was now my home. Now, in September of 2011, King and I had been together a year, but it felt like a lifetime. I said it constantly. King had changed my life. But now things were about to change even more.

"Is that a plus sign?" I was a smart girl. I studied my ass off and passed every class easily. I for damn sure could read. I definitely knew what a plus sign looked like, so I was just trying to psyche myself out.

Jada wasn't going to let that happen, though. "Your father is going to kill you."

Even in my shock and amazement, I knew better. I sucked my teeth with a hard roll of the eyes. "He won't even talk to me, so he won't make the effort to kill me, I'm sure."

Jada ignored my comment as she sat on top of the sink in the master bathroom, staring at me with critical eyes. "I told you to fuck him, not fuck up your life."

My mouth dropped to the floor as I sat on the tub. Jada was our cheerleader. If anybody had been rooting for us this entire time, it was her.

She saw the hurt in my eyes, but she didn't even apologize. "I know you love King. I know that he loves you too. I love the fact that you two are finally happy, but you're the only person–the only woman–that I know that is going to be somebody. You were supposed to be a doctor one day, girl–"

"And I still am," I replied in a tone that I didn't even believe.

"How with this baby? I'm sure King will be a good father, but you're pregnant by a nigga in the game. They don't be at home at night while the baby won't stop crying when you have to get up and go to class the next morning. And they are hardly there in the morning when it's time to get them ready for school. They are good *providers*, but they ain't there with you when you need that hands-on help."

Every word that Jada had said hit me hard upside the head like a baseball bat. While I suspected being pregnant, I had been trying to figure out what I would do if I had a baby. Jada was right; King took damn good care of me, but in order to continue to make that money, he wouldn't be able to be in the house watching a baby while I studied or went to class.

Jada saw the perplexity in my expression. "You got a lot of good things going for you, Kennedy. You're only nineteen. You have a lot of time to have babies."

All of her words added to the doubts already present in my mind about having a baby. I was dedicated to King. I was loyal to him, but I couldn't forget what I had been dedicated and loyal to before I met him. Education was my main priority before he entered my life. I was the smart girl. I wanted to be a doctor. I had aspirations of helping children, but not to give birth to them and forget about my dreams.

So that's exactly what I decided to tell King when he came home. Jada slipped out as soon as he came in because she knew that I had to have this conversation with King now. By my calculations, I had to be at least eight weeks. I had little time to toss this decision around in my mind. Plus, I didn't want to get attached to the baby if I wasn't going to keep it.

I had waited until King undressed, took his shower, and climbed into bed next to me. I usually had his nightcap waiting for him when he got out of the shower, if I was awake, so, that's what I did. The Remy was chilling on ice as he climbed into his side of the bed. Usually, I would be lying there, waiting for him to finish his drink so that he could fuck me until he was exhausted and then we would spoon until I fell asleep in those midnight colored arms. Then he would turn on the television and watch sports highlights until the sun came up.

But I knew tonight wouldn't unfold as usual. King and I had never argued before. I always listened to him, and he usually gave me what I wanted. Yet, I was sure that wanting to kill his unborn child would start our first fight.

I replayed the words over and over again in my mind, practicing so that whenever he stopped texting and gave me his undivided attention, I would be able to say them so convincingly that maybe he would understand.

"So you think you're gon' to kill my baby?"

My heart dropped to the pit of my stomach. As the words settled in the air, I felt like shit. It sounded cold, and I couldn't believe that I had ever even considered being so cold with the man that I loved more than I loved myself.

I looked at him with eyes wide with shock and fear. When he peered back into mine, the light from the television in the dark room bounced off of the tears that glossed his eyes.

"I saw the pregnancy test in the garbage can in the bathroom."

I turned from him. I couldn't stand the look of pain in his eyes. I had never seen that man so sad in his life. He was a goon. He had killed people. I was sure of it, even though he would never tell me. It looked like I was the first person to truly break his heart, and it made me feel like the smallest person on earth.

"H-how...how..." I couldn't speak around the lump in my throat. "How do you know that I don't want to keep it?"

He wouldn't even look me in the eyes. He kept his eyes on his phone as his jaws clenched tightly with frustration. "Since you're not sitting here wearing a smile, I guess you have the nerve to want to get rid of it."

I was so dumb. If I couldn't even break the news of my pregnancy maturely, how in the hell was I supposed to be somebody's mother while working toward my degree? I couldn't face him. I just threw my face into my hands and started to weep out of shame. King had never hurt me. He had always put my needs first. And the one time that I was tested, I failed, and I was selfish.

Even when I felt his arms around me, I continued to feel like shit. He even kissed the top of my head, and that didn't make it any better. "I'm sorry," I cried.

Taking my head into his hands, he put my head on his chest. I instantly wrapped my arms so tight around his body that I felt myself squeezing his ribs.

As he rubbed my hair, he asked me, "Are you scared? Is that why you don't want to keep the baby? You don't think I'll be here for you?"

"I-I-I-" I was stuttering like a fucking imbecile. I couldn't think of the right words to say that wouldn't make me look like a further fool, as even the attempted words came out wrong because tears were all over them. Plus, I knew that any excuse would make me look even more stupid, because as he held me in his arms, I knew that he would always be there to take care of me and mine.

"Haven't I always been here for you, baby?" He was speaking into my hair as he leaned over. I imagined that his heart was heavy because, for the first time in our relationship, I didn't trust him.

"Yes," I admitted as I squeezed tighter. "You've always been here for me. That's why I love you so much."

"So why wouldn't I-"

"I don't know! I wasn't thinking! I'm sorry. I was just scared. I'm only nineteen. Being your woman is enough responsibility. Then I have school. But being a mother, the mother of *your* child...I'm so young. I want to do it right. I want to do *everything* right."

He started to rock me, and I closed my eyes and enjoyed the comfort. "You'll be okay. Long as you got me, you'll always be okay. I've never left you before, and I damn sure ain't gon' leave you now."

And I believed him. With every inch of my body, with every fiber of my being, I believed him.

KING

The next morning, Meech, Dolla, and I went to meet up with Gustavo. After six months of stacking bread, we were finally ready to approach him with an offer so that we could expand our business. We had all been eager to get the shit cracking because it was going to take our business to the next level. But now I had even more pressing intentions. I was about to be a father for the first time in my life. Suddenly, the game looked different to me. It appeared to be a threat that might take me away from the two people that meant the most in the world to me. I was ready to stack my bread as high as possible so that I could retire early as a legitimate, carefree man so that I could enjoy my family.

Gustavo owned a few clubs in the city. They were businesses that he used to clean his money. That particular day we met him at Outlandish, his most popular joint on the north side of Chicago. We had arrived before it opened for the day.

"Meech, Dolla, King, come in," he said, ushering us into his office. He gave the bodyguard that followed us upstairs the okay with his eyes, indicating that he could leave us alone. The guy was hesitant at first, but Gustavo waved his hand that was filled with flawless diamonds on every finger. "¿No oyes? ¡Lárgate !" (Can't you hear?! Get the fuck out!)Then Gustavo slammed the door in his face.

He turned to us with a smile on his face and his arms outstretched. He hugged each of us, which is what he'd always done and what niggas from the hood had gradually become used to.

"Sit," he insisted, walking back to his desk wearing an all-black, slim fit suit that I was pretty sure cost thousands. Every time Gustavo met with us during his trips to Chicago, he was fresh to fucking death, almost persuading me to give up my True Religions for a suit and tie...*almost.*

We all got comfortable in the leather wingback chairs across from his desk. Before starting our meeting, he reached into his desk and pulled out two stogies and offered one to Meech. He was the only one of us that smoked those stank ass thangs.

"It's His Majesty's Reserve," Gustavo told Meech, in his thick Spanish accent. "It's made from eighteen-year-old tobacco and soaked in the most expensive cognac. Twenty-five thousand dollars a box. There's a three-year waiting list for these. Enjoy."

Meech simply nodded and slipped it into the pocket of his jacket. I imagined he would enjoy that motherfucka on his patio with a drink later on tonight.

"Now," Gustavo started as he lit the stogie and leaned back in his chair. "How may I help you, gentlemen?"

I didn't beat around the bush. I got right down to business. "We want to expand business, which means we'll need more supply...lots of it."

We all sat on pins and needles waiting for his answer. Expanding business wasn't just cut and dry. It didn't mean just putting more money in Gustavo's pocket because we were buying more product. It meant putting him at a greater risk because he would be moving more weight. We would be selling to buyers that we hadn't quite gained loyalty from and vice versa. They could get pinched and snitch. They could try to rob us. It was a gamble, so I didn't press when it took Gustavo a moment to respond.

"Where are you expanding to?" he finally asked.

"The Carolinas and further south when the opportunity presents itself, which I'm sure it will."

"You have connects down there? A plan?"

"Everything is ready to roll. We have buyers ready to cop from us. We have men set up down there and a location for the drops. We just need the product."

"And you have the money too, I assume?" he asked with a smile.

And I met his smile. "Of course."

He sat simmering in his thoughts for a few seconds, meeting each set of our confident eyes with his questioning baby blue ones. Then he locked eyes with me. "Estoes un riesgogrande, Rey." (This is a big risk, King.)

I nodded in agreement. "Estoy preparado para asegurarse de que cualquier riesgo se convierte en nada de ganancia para todos nosotros." (I'm prepared to make sure that any risk turns into nothing but gain for all of us.)

He chuckled. "Estoy seguro." (I'm sure.) Then his hands met one another at his lips as he peered over them at each one of us. "When I met you boys a few years ago, you were hungry and passionate. And you still are. That's why I like you. But more weight means more risk and more opportunities for something to fall through the cracks. Let me think about it. Give me some time?"

I could feel Meech and Dolla's disappointment, but I knew that Gustavo would come around. He'd done the same thing when we approached him with a sweeter deal than our connect was giving him. We had convinced him then, and I knew that we had convinced him now.

"Sure," I told him as I stood. "Take all the time you need."

****

After the meeting with Gustavo, I was ready to get back to the crib with my babies. I had convinced Kennedy to keep the baby, so I had to fulfill my promises to be there for her. So I was intent on spending every free moment that I could with her.

We'd all ridden in Meech's car to Outlandish, so when we got back to his crib, we stepped inside to chop it up about some other pending business matters before Dolla and I split. When we all walked in on Siren cooking in the kitchen, she looked like she'd seen a ghost. I didn't know why. It was no secret that Meech had been hitting that for the past six months. They had never been together around the crew, but Meech never left one detail untold about hitting that when it came to me and Dolla. From day one, the first night that he took her out, the nigga was bragging about hitting that pussy. She'd given it up day one and had been on a regular for six months.

I thought it was funny as hell as Siren fidgeted, suddenly uncomfortable, as Meech, oblivious to it all, walked right up on her. He wrapped his arms around her and kissed her cheek. "Hey, baby."

Of course, I had to be an asshole. "Awwww!" Then I put extra sauce on it as I sat on a stool at the island. "Y'all so cute."

Meech and Dolla chuckled, but Siren looked like she had swallowed her own shit. Still Meech was oblivious to it as he took tops off of the pots on the hot stove and peered inside. "Damn, this shit smells good. Let me go wash my hands." He then turned toward me and Dolla. "Y'all staying to eat? She can throw down."

"Nah, I'm straight," I answered. "Kennedy can throw down too, and I need to get home to that."

Instantly, Siren turned her face away from us, focusing on absolutely nothing in the refrigerator.

"Well, Jada ain't cooked in a week. A nigga been eating McDonalds," Dolla snickered. "I'm staying. Let me go wash my hands." When he left the kitchen, Meech followed to do the same.

I called after them, "I'm out, my niggas. We can chop it up tomorrow. I'll holla."

"A'ight, bro," I heard Meech shout back.

"One, bruh," Dolla returned. "Holla at me tomorrow, especially if you hear from Gustavo."

I stood to leave, not even making eye contact with Siren. She was silent, but I could hear her footsteps. Just when I thought the coast was clear, Siren stopped me as I was walking out of the kitchen. She gently grabbed my arm, saying, "King, wait."

I gave her a simple and dry, "What's up?"

"I...um...me and Meech..." She fidgeted with her clothes like a child scared to tell the truth to her father. "I mean... this ain't–"

I stopped her, putting her out of her misery. "Aye, you don't have to explain shit to me. It's cool." With each lifeless and emotionless word that left my lips, her face contorted from embarrassed to straight up pissed off. "I'm glad it worked out for him. He told me that he was feeling you a long time ago."

Her eyes grew with wonder. "He did?"

"Yeah. He asked my opinion, and I told him to make his move."

Now her eyes were full of shock. "*Really?*"

"Yeah. Why wouldn't I?"

My carelessness was pissing her off more and more. She stood in front of me with her arms folded across her big, perky, 34 DD's, shaking her head in disbelief. "Tuh," she grunted. "You really have no fucking feelings for me, huh?"

"What?" My face twisted in confusion. "You're standing in my fam's kitchen cooking. Why do you give a fuck about whether I have feelings for you or not?"

"Because you set me out to your boy like I was some hoe!" she whispered harshly, through gritted teeth.

"I didn't set you out. I put you on. He's a good dude–"

"But I wanted *you*! You knew that! All the shit I've done for you. Moving dope. Co–"

"I didn't ask you to start doing that."

"But I wanted to because I was down for you. I was ride or fucking die for you, King."

"Because you wanted the life, not me, and now you have it. You're welcome."

A landslide of bullshit was about to come from her throat in reaction, but luckily for me, Meech and Dolla returned just in time.

"You still here?" Meech asked with a smile. "Want some of this fye ass food, don't you?"

"Nah, I was just telling Siren that we should plan a couple's dinner. The girls would like that corny ass shit."

Siren forced a smile as she went back to the stove. "Yeah, that will be cool," she said.

"I'll make sure she plans that shit then," Meech nodded in agreement.

"A'ight, bro. I'm out. For real this time."

As I walked out, I fought the urge to shake my head in disgust. Siren thought she knew love. She thought she knew loyalty, but she didn't. If she did, she would have never jumped on the first opportunity to be a kept woman. She didn't love me. She loved the life. She thought she loved me, but if she did, she would respect my family, instead of being some selfish, thirsty bitch. She was acting like some needy, psycho chick. I knew that she wasn't *that* crazy, though. She may have wanted me, but now that she had that life, she wouldn't risk losing it by telling our dirty little secret.

September 2011

CHAPTER FOURTEEN

KENNEDY

A few days after finding out that I was pregnant, the fear and anxiety finally went away, and excitement settled in. I was going to be a mother but not just any mother. I would be the mother of King's first born child.

Finally, it appeared that my dreams were coming true. I had the man of my dreams. He spoiled me rotten. Now we were going to be a family. I was on a natural high. I was higher than cloud nine. But when I walked into my mother's house to tell her the good news, I was thrown off of that cloud just as fast as I'd climbed on it.

"Oh my goodness!" she squealed. The smile on her face was bright as we sat close to one another on the couch. "I'm going to be a grandmother! Aw!"

I smiled as a sigh of relief escaped me. I thought that she would be upset or disappointed, but she wasn't. As always, she supported me in any and everything. She didn't even judge me when I moved out of her house and into King's. She had insisted that I follow my heart because King was a good man that took really good care of me. I think she went overboard with the support because she knew that for so many years she hadn't been there for me every day like she'd wanted to be. She knew that although my environment was better, emotionally living with my father was a pain back then, and she carried a lot of guilt for losing me to him.

My mother noticed the peculiar smile on my face and asked, "What's wrong?"

"I thought you would be disappointed," I admitted.

She sucked her teeth and waved her hand as if I was being so silly. "Girl, please. Why would I be disappointed?"

"Because I'm so young, and I'm in school."

"You aren't the first teenager to get pregnant. And I know you. You are a smart girl, and you're responsible. I know you're still going to finish school and become the doctor that you've always wanted to be so you can help children."

I smiled as her words sunk in.

Then she had to say the words that took my smile away instantly. "I'm not the one that you have to worry about. You know I got you. Your father is the one that you have to worry about."

My heart sunk with the realization that she was correct.

"Are you going to tell him?

"He still won't talk to me." A ball of frustration and sadness grew in my throat so large that I could hardly breathe. At this point, I had given up trying to reach out to my father, but it hurt me every day that he had allowed something so miniscule to come between us. He got on my gawd damn nerves, but I still had the desire in my heart to make him smile with pride. This baby was going to make that smile vanish completely if it wasn't gone already.

My mother saw the sadness in my eyes and put her arms around me. "Your father is stubborn as hell. Shit, that's why I left his ass." Her faint chuckle didn't do its job of making me laugh. "Just prove him wrong, baby," she insisted. "Prove him wrong. And smile! You're having a baby! And it can feel your energy, ya know? You hungry?"

Even though I told her, "No, King and I are supposed to go to dinner later," she again waved her hand like I was being silly and stood up.

"You gotta feed that baby. Ain't nothing wrong with eating twice."

"Mama," I whined. "Just because I'm pregnant don't mean I have to get fat."

"Well, if you don't want to get fed, you might not want to come over here. But you're here now, so you finna eat. I'll be back. I got some leftover smothered chicken and rice from last night. Let me warm it up."

I didn't even bother to protest as she headed out of the living room. There was no arguing with her. She was going to force feed me if she had to.

"Oh!" She stopped at the end table nearby and grabbed some mail off of it. "You got a bunch of mail over here."

She handed it to me and was gone to warm up that food that would make my hips spread even more. I smiled at my mother's excitement as I realized that she was about to act like this was her baby. I sorted through the mail with a warm feeling. I didn't have my father's consent, but King and my mother were so happy that they were making up for it and then some.

"Oh my God," I whispered as one of the pieces of mail caught my eyes. It was from Spelman. I had forgotten all about applying months back when King told me to. "Mama! How long has this mail been here?"

"For a little while," I heard her say from the kitchen.

Now I was descending from my cloud. I had been so wrapped up in wondering if I was pregnant that looking for the response from Spelman had completely slipped my mind.

I took a deep breath as I tore the envelope open. I didn't feel one way or the other about what the letter could say. If I was accepted, I couldn't go. There was no way that I could go to Atlanta with a baby. I couldn't imagine being away from King or taking his baby away from him either.

"Kennedy, you hear me?"

I guess I hadn't, but I still couldn't respond because I was engulfed in reading the letter.

"Kennedy?"

Congratulations! It is my pleasure to offer you admission to Spelman College for the fall 2011...

That was all that I needed to read. I closed my eyes, and a smile spread across my cheeks as tears slid from up under my eyelids.

"Kennedy, what's wrong?"

I finally realized that my mother had come into the living room. When I tore my eyes open, she was taking the letter from my hands. It only took her a few seconds before her reaction pierced the air. "Ahhhh! Yes! Oh my God!"

She was jumping up and down for joy, but when she realized that I wasn't, she stopped and looked at me like I was crazy. "What's wrong?!"

"I can't go, Mama! I'm pregnant!"

The excitement of my acceptance had made her forget just that fast. The realization took the joy from her eyes, and she looked at me with sympathy.

"It's okay," I insisted as I wiped my eyes. "I'm just happy that I got in."

She moved toward me with open arms, but I stopped her embrace as I stood. "Really, Ma, it's fine. Let's go eat."

****

"Fuck you mean you not goin'?" King looked at me like I was crazy as we sat across from one another at Ruth's Chris Steakhouse.

As we waited for the appetizers, I had told him about my mother's overboard reaction to my baby, how she stuffed my face with smothered chicken and my acceptance to Spelman.

"I can't go obviously," I told him.

And he continued to look at me like he didn't understand. "Why not?"

"What do you mean 'why not'? I'm pregnant, King. I know a lot of women go to college with babies, but I don't want to leave you, and I am definitely not taking your first child away from you. That's selfish."

"But Spelman is your dream."

"And I got accepted. At least I can say that. And I'm in school. I'm still following the career path that I wanted to, and that's good enough for me."

As I said it, I knew it was bullshit. The desire to go to Spelman was still burning in my heart like hot lava, but my motherly instincts had already kicked in, on top of my feelings for King.

Love for my family was trumping my desires to live out my dreams on the campus of Spelman.

King saw that it was bullshit too. "That's not good enough for you, and you know it."

He smiled to make his argument more soothing, and it worked. Sitting over there with his locs twisted in an intricate design and his earrings glowing like the sun, I couldn't help but laugh and tell the truth. "You're right. I really wanna go, but I can't." Then I poked my bottom lip out.

"Yes, you can," he told me as he reached across the table and held my hand. "We can still keep the same plan like before. I'll just go with you." I watched him with wide, eager eyes as he continued to be the man that he had always been to me: loving me, spoiling me, and giving me everything I wanted. "*We* can move down there...the three of us."

I looked at him timidly, wondering if he was serious. "What about your business?"

He shrugged his shoulders like the idea was nothing. Like leaving the only place and people that he'd known as home was no big deal. "I can fly back and forth when necessary. Plus, if Gustavo gives us the extra product that we need to expand, it'll be good to be closer to the new set-up down south." King watched me as I took it all in and slowly started to get excited. "It'll be great," he continued to seal the deal as he squeezed my hand.

"I can't believe you're willing to do that for me." I smiled.

"I love you, baby...all of you, especially the intelligent, educated you. And *that* girl wants to go to Spelman, so she's going."

I let out a big sigh of relief as I said, "Okay. But I want to wait until I have the baby. I am guessing my due date will be sometime in April or May. The doctor will tell me for sure at my appointment in a few weeks. That way my mother can be around during my pregnancy and then we'll have time to move before the fall semester starts next year."

King was happy. He grinned proudly at me. He was proud that I was still the smart, ambitious girl that he'd fallen in love with. "Good. It's a plan." Then he squeezed my hand and kissed it, saying reassuringly, "Everything is going to work out."

King

On the way home from dinner, I got a call from Gustavo. He was approving our expansion. So I dropped Kennedy off at the crib and went straight to Meech's house, where Dolla already was as well, to tell them the good news.

"It's on, my niggas!" Meech shouted after we discussed the specifics. With a grin full of the anticipation of more money, he held his glass of Patron up awaiting our toast.

Dolla and I toasted him. We all sat around the island with feelings of pride. I had started this organization, but Meech and Dolla had been influential and intricate parts of it. It was very much theirs as it was mine. We had grown from selling rocks and blows to being the sole distributors for many cities in the Midwest and now we were moving into the south.

Things were looking great. Life couldn't have been better, so I decided to tell my boys even more good news. "Kennedy's having my baby."

As soon as the words left my mouth, Meech and Dolla's eyes bucked. Meech nearly spit out his tequila.

"*What?*" Dolla shouted. "King finally got got!"

I chuckled. "Man, whatever. She didn't *get* me."

"I know, nigga, but I'm just saying. You know how many bitches wanna have your baby? You've dodged the bullet for years."

"Nah, I just strapped the fuck up, unlike you."

"Aye, whatever," Dolla laughed. "At least I got mine out the way early. Now you about to be runnin' around after toddlers in your thirties. That shit is whack."

I smiled proudly at the thought. "I'm looking forward to it, though."

"Well, I ain't," Meech replied.

"You ain't tryin' to have no shorties with Siren?" Dolla asked.

"Not now. I didn't think being a father was so much responsibility until Siren and Elijah moved in. I don't know if I'm ready for that with my own seed."

"Elijah's father still ain't stepped up?" I asked.

"Hell nah. That nigga don't call and don't show. Didn't send the little nigga nothing for his birthday or Christmas." When he shook his head with a clenched jaw, I realized just how much Meech really fucked with Siren. He cared for her so much that he cared for her son. He was a father to him, and that was what was up. I thought about how she acted the other night and felt sorry for her. She had blown my phone up all night, but I sent her dumb ass to voicemail. She had a good nigga at the crib that was taking care of her and her shorty, but she still found interest in stalking me. The shit was sad. She didn't even realize what a good dude she had because she was so fucking obsessed with me.

"That shit is crazy. He's a punk ass nigga for that shit," Dolla said.

"Tell me about it. I see that nigga all the time when I go play ball out west with my cousin. They went to school together. Motherfucka be fresh to deaf, but won't even send his son a pair of Jays. The shit is crazy."

"You ain't never checked that nigga?" Dolla asked.

"Nah. When I told Siren that I wanted to holla at him, she asked me not to. She don't even want the nigga to think that she needs him, and I can't blame her for that." Dolla and I agreed with a nod. "But I hope she changes her mind one day. I'd love to put my foot in his ass."

Jessica N. Watkins

APRIL 2012

Chapter Fifteen

Kennedy

Seven months after deciding to go to Spelman, I was in full blown labor.

"Arrrrgh!"

"Push!" I heard the doctor urging. "Come on, Kennedy! You're almost there."

"Ahhhh!" I was screaming for dear life. I was so loud that I was sure that our friends and family could hear me as they sat in the waiting area of the University of Chicago's maternity ward. I had gone into labor almost three hours ago. I was snatched out of my sleep when I felt a pain down my back that *had* to be killing me. By the time the second contraction was coming, King was trying to help me put on my clothes. By the third, he was guiding me out into the new springtime morning sun and hurriedly ushering me into his new Cadillac ATS, which he called his "family car" since it was a sedan.

On our way to the hospital, King notified my mother and Meech that I was in labor. By the time we arrived at the hospital, everyone was waiting for us. My mother, Meech, Dolla, Jada, Siren were all present. His mother and both of our fathers were of course absent. King didn't know his father, his mother was a drug addict that lost custody of him when he was four, and my father still wasn't speaking to me. I hadn't even told him about my pregnancy. I felt guilty about it, until my mother told me that when she called my father to tell him, he told her that I would end up being the same kind of mother she was and hung up on her.

"Okay, relax," Dr. Harris told me. "Catch your breath before another contraction comes."

There was a nurse on each side of me, holding one of my legs. They were wide open. My mother was standing behind me, soothing me with words of encouragement. And King was all over the room, videotaping the delivery as he asked the nurses and doctor a million gawd damn questions. In the jogging pants that he had slept in and a wife beater, he looked so sweet and naïve. Unless he was smiling into my eyes, he always came off as a dangerous, not to be fucked with gangsta. Today, he was smiling from ear to ear, and the naivety was all over him. He was having a baby, and it was new to him. The anticipation and nervousness was oozing from him.

"Ahhh!" Another contraction was coming. I looked at my mother for help, but all she could do was wipe my forehead with the icy cold towel. "King, would you put that damn phone down?!"

My irate tone had had no effect on his mood. He kept that goofy ass grin on his face and the phone up in the air. "I gotta record every moment, baby."

"Push, Kennedy!" The nurses put me back into focus. "Come on."

"I see the head!" I heard King say. "Oh shit!"

"Arrrrgh!" I was pushing for dear life; pushing past the pain, while watching King watch his baby come out of me with eyes the size of saucers. "Arrrrgh!"

"That's it, Kennedy! Push!" Dr. Harris urged. "Here comes the shoulders!"

****

Kayla Denise King was seven pounds, three ounces, and nineteen inches long. She was the most beautiful baby in the world, and if you tried to tell King otherwise, he would kill you–literally.

"Look at all that curly hair," Jada said nearly in a whisper as she leaned over me, tracing Kayla's cheek with her finger. Siren was behind her staring at Kayla. Surprisingly, I saw tears in her eyes. I knew that it was an emotional occasion, but Siren's tears seemed a bit dramatic. But Kayla's face would bring anyone to tears; she was just that beautiful.

I was holding Kayla close to my chest. It had been two hours since she was born, and now everyone was in my hospital room, eyeing her and taking pictures. King stood next to me proudly as my mother took tons of pictures of *everybody*. She was *so* excited.

"Yeeeeah," I practically sang, as I stared at Kayla dreamingly. "She has that thick, black hair like King."

"She looks *just* like you, though," I heard Carla say, and it was true. Kayla looked like a spitting image of my newborn pictures, which my mom had shown everybody.

"She does," left my lips in the most adoring tone. I was mesmerized by my baby as I played in her curly mane. I was sure that my hair looked the same as hers; all over my head. I was in such a hurry to leave that morning that I hadn't even put as much as my fingers through it. I damn sure didn't touch a comb. The residue of the labor was all over me. I looked tired and a mess, but the smile on my face was just as beautiful as Kayla's face.

I closed my eyes when I felt King's fingers running through my hair. When he bent down and kissed my forehead, I wanted to just fall asleep right then. I was exhausted from the labor and delivery, but I forced myself to stay awake when I heard King say, "Baby."

Before I could open my eyes, I heard lots of gasps, so I shot them open. I was met with everyone's eyes staring wildly toward me but not at me. I looked over and didn't see King. Then I looked down and saw that he was on one knee.

"Ah!" I screamed as my eyes filled with tears. My eyes darted to everyone in the room, searching for confirmation that this was really happening. My mama looked at me with the most pleased smile on her face, giving me that nurturing nod. Dolla and Meech's faces were behind phones as they took picture after picture. Jada stood on the other side of me with the same smile as my mother. She was happy for me just as my mother was. She had always been. Siren seemed just as shocked at the proposal as I was. Her eyes were just as wide as mine as she had a surprised smirk as she stared at King. And when I looked at King, if I didn't know it was real, I then was positive that it was because he was retrieving a black, velvet box from his pocket.

I lost it! "Oh my God! Oh!" I almost forgot that I was holding my baby. Jada took her from me just in time for me to throw my hands over my face. I could hear Dolla and Meech cheering on their boy as many female voices squealed in delight.

I felt King grab my wrists and take my hands away from my face. Camera flashes blinded me, but I could see that everyone in the room had stood to take pictures as nurses stuck their heads in the room.

"Kennedy, I'm not going to say some long ass corny speech," he chuckled. "But before I met you, I would have never guessed that I'd be back here on one knee, asking another woman to marry me. But you showed me that my queen, my Reina, was real. She's *you*. And I want this...us...for the rest of my life. Will you marry me?"

The ring that he was holding in the air was just as beautiful as this day. The three karat diamond ring set in platinum was exquisite and expensive, but worth more than all the money in the world was the man peering up at me lovingly through gorgeous, sultry, bedroom eyes.

We had only been together a little over a year now. There hadn't been much to our relationship. There had been no drama, no cheating, and few arguments. It was simple, but that was because our love for each other was real, and the loyalty ran deep. For so long I had been infatuated with a love that I thought came with cheating, fighting bitches, and court cases, along with the street nigga, but I had gotten the complete opposite in King. He took care of me emotionally, physically, and spiritually without me having to beg, complain or curse. Because of that alone, and besides all of the other reasons that I loved him, I wanted nothing else in this world but to be his wife.

But I couldn't even form those words. So I just cried like my newborn baby and nodded.

And the room went up in hysterics.

KING

I slipped the ring on Kennedy's finger as best as I could. I was a nigga that had been in a lot of bullshit in my life. I had killed niggas, robbed niggas and made business deals with foreign niggas. But none of those situations made me as nervous as I was right then. Camera phones continued to flash as I stood and bent over to kiss my wife. In my mind, she had been my wife a little while after I met her. She was just right for me. I was going to marry Tiana back then because I felt like I should have because I owed her that. But I was going to marry Kennedy for *me*. I didn't want to live my life much longer without her being connected to me for the rest of my life.

"I love you," I told her as I wiped her tears.

"I love you too. I love you *so much*."

Even with a face full of tears and her hair all over her head, Kennedy hadn't been sexier to me than right then at that very moment. She wasn't a challenge. She didn't argue back. She didn't curse me out. She was the total opposite of everything I thought that I wanted and every fucking thing that I needed.

"Good!" I heard Dolla say. "I still got my suit from the last gawd damn wedding."

Everyone broke out into laughter so loud that you would have thought that we were at Jokes and Notes or some shit. Even Kennedy started to laugh through her tears, and once I put my pride to the side, I admitted the shit was funny too by laughing as well.

"Good, motherfucka!" I shot back at Dolla.

Just then, Kayla started to whine, so Jada brought her back to Kennedy. As Kennedy took her in her arms, I literally slid into the bed next to them. I could have stayed there for the rest of my life. Outside of the bed was mayhem and chaos. My home life was peaceful, but my business created a lot of mayhem. We had been able to control it and keep it at a minimum, but it was stressful being the head of an organization that fed so many people. I would have liked to lie in that bed with those two beautiful ladies for the rest of my life, but eventually, I had to head back into the chaos to feed them.

****

"Are you fucking kidding me, King?!"

I jumped. Siren had completely caught me off guard as I was coming out of the men's bathroom.

"Are you fucking serious?! You just don't give one fuck, do you?!"

"What the fuck are you talking about?" I looked frantically up and down the hall. Luckily, the bathroom was way down the hall on the opposite side of the ward. But still, Siren had never had this look in her eyes, and she had never been so loud knowing that others were around somewhere.

"You know what the fuck I'm talking about! You're marrying her?!"

"Hell yeah," I answered with a chuckle. "Fuck you mean? That's my lady. What the fuck is wrong with you?"

She blew a heavy breath and ran her fingers through her hair. "I gotta watch you marry another bitch?"

"Huh? I watch you be under my boy every day."

"That's because you don't want me! That's *only* because you don't want me."

I was stunned. Ashton Kutcher had to be somewhere hiding behind one of the doors because he had to be punking a nigga. There should've been no way that this chick was checking for me. I hadn't talked to Siren since the day that I was standing in Meech's kitchen. She had started calling me so much that I had to put her on the block list. When we were forced to be around each other whenever we all hung out, it was a hi-and-bye situation. But all of us were hanging out less and less lately. Me, Dolla, and Meech had been so busy with setting up the organization down south that we didn't have time for group dates and shit.

"Are you fucking serious right now?" I looked at her, waiting for her to tell me that this shit was a joke. I was also waiting for her to congratulate me on my newborn daughter and my engagement. I could deal with her obsession with me before, but now the shit was just odd. She was straight. She had the hustler that she always wanted. Now that the connect had supplied us with the necessary quantity we needed to start our organization down south, money was rolling in like never before. We thought we were balling before, but now that we were supplying them niggas down south, money was raining on us. Money was flooding in like rough waters. Now that we had expanded our business, Dolla, Meech, and I had plans on expanding our personal lives with new cars, homes, and new businesses to clean and multiply our money. Therefore, Siren should have been good. She should have been happy while she shopped for a bigger crib with Meech and bought fancy ass expensive shit to furnish that motherfucka while she was driving around in that foreign car that he'd just bought her. She had a good life with a good nigga.

She should have been happy, but she wasn't. "Yes! Yes, I'm serious, King!"

"Siren, we haven't fucked around in over a year." I was talking to her like I was talking to a child, how I imagined I would talk to Kayla once she was older and I was trying to talk some sense into her. "You're with my boy, my best motherfucking friend."

"So! Feelings don't just go away like that, King!"

This chick was blowing my mind. I had to lean against the wall in order to brace myself and take all of this shit in. "What feelings?"

"My feelings for *you*. Don't act stupid, King."

"I never told you to have feelings for me! It's not my fault that you thought what you was getting from me was more than dick. I'm supposed to make my decisions based on your feelings because you caught them when you wasn't fucking supposed to?"

She looked crushed. Right there in that hallway I knew that I had broken her heart into unrepairable pieces. I had never fed her the truth like that...that raw. I had always just dodged her or avoided her, but obviously her delusional ass needed to hear that shit plain, fucking simple and real clear. "I never wanted you–*never*. You're crazy as fuck if you think I did. I never wanted to be with you. I never made you feel that way. Half the time, I didn't want to fuck you, but I did because you was there. You was fun, ma. Yeah, you're a good friend. Yeah, you hold it down for my squad. But I never wanted to be with you. I never thought about you in that way–*never*."

Her heart was sinking with every word. With every word, her anger was turning into sorrow, but I couldn't have compassion for her. You can't sympathize with crazy, and she was absolutely insane if she was standing in this hallway asking me why I was marrying my woman that had just had my baby while her nigga was in the other room.

SIREN

"...You was fun, ma. Yeah, you're a good friend. Yeah, you hold it down for my squad. But I never wanted to be with you. I never thought about you in that way–*never*."

I never knew that it was possible for him to cause any worse hurt than he already had, but I knew now. Being dismissed by some random ass nigga is one thing, but being dismissed by the friend that you are in love with was heart wrenching.

"How could you say that?" My bark had lost all bite. Standing in front him, I felt like an insecure, simple bitch that wanted nothing more than to show him how worthy I was of being his woman.

"It's the truth, Siren. You know what it was."

"And you know what it was! You know that I love you!"

His eyes bucked. "Love me?" He sighed deeply as he ran his hand over his locs. He was frustrated. I had never seen him show me this much emotion. And even though it wasn't the emotions that I wanted, it oddly made me feel better. Finally, this motherfucka saw me. He saw me as more than just his fuck buddy that did anything for him. He saw me as the woman that loved him, whether he liked it or not.

"Why are you telling me this now?" he asked me. "My woman just had my baby. I just proposed to her."

"That's supposed to be *me* in that room! *I'm* supposed to be her. *I'm* supposed to be your queen!"

He watched my oncoming tears with sympathy. His empathy made this even more evident for me. He felt sorry for my feelings for him because he was not willing to do anything about them.

He shook his head slowly as he looked at me and simply said, "I'm sorry," before walking away.

So many things went through my mind as I watched him sway past me in the sexy, masculine way that he always walked. I wanted to chase after him and beat the shit out of him for using me for years, and for never thinking I was good enough to be Mrs. Carter. I also wanted to kick his ass for just pushing me off on his boy like he was getting rid of his "problem." But I also wanted to run after him, wrap my arms around his waist and beg him to stay and to choose me and give me a chance.

That's all I had ever wanted. While I was fucking and sucking him and cooking and running dope for him, that was all I ever wanted. I just wanted him to give me a chance. But now I knew that he was never even willing to do that because he never saw me. He saw the pussy, the favors, and the friendship, but he never saw me as the woman who loved him too much, almost dangerously. I had done so much for him in his name, because of my love for him... much more than he knew now, and more than he probably would ever know.

Present day

Four days after release

CHAPTER SIXTEEN

MEECH

"Pat, my nigga, what's up?" I had to look at the phone twice. I couldn't believe that it was my cousin, Pat, from out west. Pat wasn't a street nigga. He had gone to college and become an engineer. We started to lose touch when he graduated from college four years ago. His professional life superseded the weekend basketball games that we used to play. Then two years ago, he'd gotten this new cushy position at some firm in New York, so he was really busy and barely ever in town.

"You tell me, *Money Bags*. Heard you been in Chicago killin' 'em!"

That was true. For the past three years, money was coming in so fast that the shit was almost scary. At first, it was coming in slowly. But once Kennedy got locked up, that nigga, King, had put all of his energy into his hustle. It was like he wanted to make sure that Kennedy came home to a fairytale, like he wanted to make all of her suffering worth it. And he had. It was a fairytale for all of us. It was like a dream. Too fucking good to be true. My family and I were happy, especially those in my home, Siren and Elijah.

"Yeah," I said with a confident smile as I leaned back on the couch. "Shit's pretty good out here. How 'bout you?"

"Shit is great for me, man."

"I see. You living that good life in New York. What's up, man?"

"I'm in town for like two days. Had to shoot here unexpectedly. My wife's mother isn't doing too good."

"Man, sorry to hear that."

"I know, but it gives me a chance to hook up with my people. So what's up? You down for an old school game of ball or what?"

That sounded good. My mind had been so deep in selling dope, dealing with murder investigations, and taking care of disloyal niggas that I hadn't really had the chance to be Meech. Besides, I had been in the crib alone all day anyway. Siren had taken Elijah out on a "play date," and now that we had taken care of Lock, there was no significant business to handle that day. "That's what's up."

"Cool! Meet me there in about an hour."

"Cool. One."

****

Two hours later, I was whooping Pat's ass! The score was twenty-two to three in a one-on-one game.

"Yeah, nigga," I taunted him after shooting yet another three. "I see your ass done fell off over the years." He had. He'd left Chicago with a six-pack and came back looking like he was carrying a six-month-old fetus.

"Fuck you, Meech," he breathed heavily. "This just practice, nigga."

"Yeah, you better get your shit together. Stop embarrassing yourself in front of these ladies."

The gym at the recreation center was where everyone went to play ball. Chicks knew that, so they acted like they had some business in here just to be seen. Though there was only one other one-on-one game happening at the other end of the court, there were about six ladies standing around watching.

"Oh shit! What up, Pat?"

I stopped dribbling as we heard a familiar voice.

Get the fuck outta here. I couldn't believe it. It was Eric, Elijah's father. I tried hard not to instantly go in on this nigga as he walked up to us looking like new money. For years, I had done as Siren asked and not said shit to him about the way he played Elijah. At first, it was easy for me to do. Siren was a friend, but it also wasn't my business. Once she became my woman, it got harder and harder not to check this nigga as I filled his shoes. I was happy to do it, but as Elijah got older and wanted to know why his real father wouldn't fuck with him that shit fucked with me. Elijah wasn't blood, but he was my son, and nobody hurts my son.

Luckily for Eric, I hadn't seen him in years, but as he chopped it up with Pat, I tried to remain cool out of respect for Siren's wishes.

"Damn, E, I ain't seen you in a long time, fam," Pat told him as they shook up. "What's been up?"

"Chillin', man. Out here doing my thing, ya' know?"

I had to bite my tongue as I eyed this motherfucker's confidence. He was standing here like he wasn't the worst father in the world...like his own son didn't have his fucking phone number or even know his name, for that matter.

"Oh, shit. What's up Meech?"

He reached out to shake my hand, but I simply gave his ass the head nod. He looked offended, but he knew better than to say something about it. We were from two different sides of town, but my reputation was statewide, along with King's and Dolla's. I was sure that it was our drugs that had financed his Rolex, leather jacket, Balmain gear, and Givenchy sneakers. This motherfucka had on over ten thousand dollars' worth of clothes, but hadn't sent Elijah as much as a gift card in the mail. I was fuming the longer I stood there.

Eric had put his attention back on Pat, ignoring the way that I was sneering at his punk ass. "What you doin' out this way, man?"

"My wife's mother is sick, so we came to town for a few days. I actually gotta get back to work the day after tomorrow. My wife is going to stay here with her mother, though."

"I'm sorry to hear that her mother is sick. Are the kids with her?"

"Yeah, my terrible twins are here too, man."

Pat had two sets of twins that were five and seven.

"I'll tell my girl to call her then. She can keep her company. You know they went to school together. Maybe they can get together and have a play date or some shit. You know I got me a little four-year-old. That motherfucka know he spoiled."

The fuck? I couldn't hold my composure no more. I looked at the bitch ass nigga like he was crazy.

Pat thought I was tripping. He looked at me curiously and asked, "You good, fam?"

Fuck it. Siren is just gon' have to be mad at me. She'll get over it. "Nah, I'm not good," I spit. Both Pat and Eric's eyes bucked in curiosity, but they were soon about to find out what the fuck was up. "I'm standing here trying to understand how this bitch ass nigga can stand here, iced out, fresh labels, bragging about spoiling a kid when I been taking care of his for years." By this time, I had thrown the ball and started walking up on Eric, ready to put my foot in his ass. "I should take all of this shit off yo' punk ass right now."

Instantly, Pat came between us. "Wait. Hold up–"

Pat got cut off when Eric stepped right back in my face. "I don't know what the fuck you talkin' about. I take care of mine!"

"Not your son, nigga! *I* take care of Elijah!"

Pat was still trying to keep us apart, but he was fighting a losing battle.

"My son's name is *Eric*, and he lives with me! I don't know what the fuck you're talkin' about," he swore, with his arms raised in surrender.

When I saw how seriously confused he looked, I backed down a little, astonished at how this motherfucka could just erase the existence of his own seed out of his mind. "*Elijah,* the baby you had with Siren six years ago. Or do you make so many shorties and leave them that you forgot?"

He was so thrown off by this shit that he had to laugh. "What the fuck are you talkin' about? I don't have a kid by Siren."

Now, I was confused. "You what?"

"Nigga, I'm serious. Straight up. We hung out back then, but I never even fucked with shorty. Literally, like I never fucked her. I ain't seen her in over six years." When he saw my confusion, his eyes widened in curiosity. "Is she sayin' she got a kid by me?"

I didn't even answer. My response was turning to leave. "Pat, I'll holla at you later."

I had some shit to take care of right fucking now.

"Meech! Where you goin'?"

Anger was simmering in me, and it was starting to boil over. I wanted to get home so bad that I literally started running out of the gym.

****

♪ *Say you getting throwed*
I'm tryna pour up with you
Oh, that's your best friend?
I'm tryna fuck her with you
First met the bitch, they said they real sisters
I don't give a fuck if they was real sisters ♪

I was speeding like a mad man as I approached the exit. So many things were going through my mind. I was so fucking pissed. I couldn't even breathe as Future blasted through the speakers of my Lexus.

Luckily, Siren was home. Her Porsche was sitting right in the driveway in its usual spot. As I parked my car and hopped out, I wanted to bust every window out of that pretty motherfucka. I was fuming!

I knew it! I fucking knew that that bitch was playing me, but I tried to give her the benefit out of the doubt!

"Siren!" I shouted as I entered the crib. "Yo', Siren! Get the f–"

"Aye! Aye!" she said running out the living room and into the foyer. "What the hell is wrong with you? Elijah is asleep!"

I was charging toward her as I asked, "Who is his father, Siren?"

Her face balled up in confusion. "What the fuck are you talking about, Meech?"

"Who is Elijah's father?"

"Eric! You–" Now that I was up on her, I snatched her by both arms, and she yelped. "Ow, Meech!"

"Don't fucking play with me, Siren!" Spit flew out of my mouth as my jaw clenched so tight that I felt like it was going to break. "Tell me! Tell me who the fuck his father is!"

As she saw the tears come to my eyes, she knew that I knew. When I saw that birthmark, I had a feeling, but I would never think that the two closest people in my life would play me like this, the two people that I loved more than myself. For years, I just hoped that maybe it was a coincidence that they both had that same signature birthmark that only the people closest to them would see since it was in such an intimate place.

"Meech...I..." she stuttered, avoiding my eyes and trying to think of more lies. "I..."

I clamped down on her arms even harder, my anger pouring out in my grip. "Siren, I swear to God! Y–"

"Mommy! Daddy!" Elijah interrupted us. He was on the stairs with the fear of God in his eyes. "Stop fighting!"

Siren and I both jumped when we heard Elijah on the stairs, but I didn't let her go. I glared into her eyes waiting for an answer.

"Please don't do this in front of him," she begged.

"Elijah, go upstairs. Everything is okay," I told him without turning to face him. "Me and your mom are just talking."

"But you're yelling."

"I'll stop. I promise."

I looked over my shoulder. When I smiled at him, he was convinced, but my heart was broken, straight up. I tried hard to hold back the one or two tears that wanted to fall as he stood for a second or two before smiling back at me and going back upstairs.

Then I turned my rage back to Siren. "Bitch, you betta start talkin'."

She looked crushed. I had never in my life called her out of her name or even put my hands on her. Shit, we had little to argue about. Life was good. We had no complaints. There had never been any disloyalty... until now.

When she continued to hesitate, I squeezed tighter, damn near breaking her arms. She started to cry, "You're hurting me, Meech."

"Start talkin'."

"Eric is–" I tightened my grip on her arms, so much so that I could feel her bones against my fingers. "Ow! Okay! Okay!" Tears streamed down her face as we stared into each other's eyes. Something told me that this was the last time that I would ever hold Siren again or even look her in the face. "King is his father."

Siren

I had been living with this lie for six years. Finally telling it was like a burden being lifted from my shoulders. But the burden was now replaced with guilt and heartache because I watched as that truth literally took all fight from Meech's body. He let me go and leaned against the wall, with his hands in his pockets and his eyes to the ceiling.

"I can't believe you motherfuckas played me."

When I said, "He doesn't know," Meech looked at me like I was crazy, but he was also relieved. I continued with the truth, "King doesn't know that Elijah is his."

When I first got pregnant with Elijah, I was so excited. I felt like finally King would choose me, and we could be a family. But then he proposed to Tiana before I could tell him that I was pregnant. I knew that his response would be to kill my baby. I loved King, but I loved my baby more, so I lied to everyone about who the father was. I used Eric's name since he and I were no longer kicking it, and no one knew him. I figured since he was from out west no one would ever cross paths with him. He was some random, no-name, street nigga that thought he was a big time hustler but was only selling no more than nickel bags of weed out of his mama's house, back then. No one would ever run into this nigga, so I thought. I could have my baby and continue on with life like it never happened. I was concerned about getting away with it once I had him, but as the years went by, there wasn't anything related to King about him, expect that fucking birthmark. It was shaped like a heart and on his back, just like King's.

Imagine my terror when Meech started seeing Eric on the West Side when he played ball. But regardless of how King treated me, on the surface we were all family. We were all loyal, so they kept their word by not confronting him like they wanted to.

"He doesn't know. I swear to God," I insisted.

"Are you serious? What the fuck is wrong with you?"

"He was marrying Tiana! He would have made me get an abortion!"

"So you was fucking around with this, nigga? For how long, Siren?"

"It was only once," I lied. "And he was so fucking drunk that he didn't even remember." I still had that loyalty to my crew. I couldn't break that bond that Meech and King had by telling him the whole truth. And even after all those years, after he'd proposed to Tiana and then married Kennedy, I was still loyal to him by not telling our secrets.

Meech looked relieved to hear that, but he was still very much pissed at me.

Then I made it worse. "Please don't tell, King." Meech looked down on me like I was pathetic. "Please? It's going to mess up everything. Kennedy just got out. Think about your business. Please, Me–"

"Get the fuck out, Siren."

My eyes bucked. "No, Meech. Pleas–"

"Get out! Now! Elijah can stay, but you gotta fucking go."

"Are you serious?"

"Dead ass! You been lying to me for years! What's worse is you been lying to Elijah!" As he whispered harshly, he came toward me, and I flinched. "You got him thinking his own father don't even want him when his father doesn't know that he has a son!"

He was dragging me toward the door, and I was fighting my exit. "Please, Meech. Don't throw me out because of this!" I was terrified. I didn't want to lose him, this life, and my happiness; not over King, not when King was happy as shit without me.

"Get the fuck out!" he insisted.

"No!" I argued as I tried to get loose from his grasp. "I'm not leaving without my son!"

"That's *my* son! You didn't love him enough to tell him the truth! So you don't deserve him, and you don't deserve me either!"

We tussled and, as we did, I fell to the floor. While I was down there, I wrapped my arms around his legs and just began to sob. "Please, Meech. I love you."

And even that was a lie. Even after all of these years, I loved King, only him and I always would. But that motherfucka had hurt me. He hadn't chosen me and because of that my son was hurting too. He was a smug bastard that didn't give a fuck about shit but his precious Kennedy, his queen! Yes, I was still protecting him, but I'd be damned if I would lose again because of him. It wasn't fair!

But Meech was so big and strong that he was still able to walk toward the door with me wrapped around his leg and sobbing. I heard the front door opening, and I knew it was over. My heart began to beat so hard and fast that I knew I was losing my life. As Meech bent down and literally pushed me on the other side of the door, I knew that I had lost this wonderful life that he had given me, and I would never get it back. But as he slammed the door, I didn't even bother to fight my way back in. He was right to kick me out. I didn't deserve this life. If he thought this secret was bad, he had no idea. The other secrets that I was keeping were deadly.

AUGUST 2012

CHAPTER SEVENTEEN

KENNEDY

By August 2012, King and I were getting ready for the big move to Atlanta. It was bittersweet. I hated to see King leave his family. They were his closest friends, and I hated to be away from the only parent that I remained in contact with. But I was excited for my future at Spelman as I began a new life with my fiancé and my four-month-old daughter.

School was starting in two weeks. So, on a Monday morning, Jada was helping me finish packing. King had hired professionals to pack up the house and had already shipped a few things to our new crib in Atlanta, including his cars, but I didn't trust those movers with my clothes and shoes. Besides King and Kennedy, they were my prized possessions, and I didn't want any their wives, girlfriends, baby mamas or daughters walking around in my shit.

♪ *Nigga, I'm three hunna... Bang*

I'm coolin with my youngins

And what we smoke one hunna

But nigga I'm three hunna

Click Clack, Pow, now he runnin'

Don't be fuckin with my youngins

Them niggas be drummin'

They take ya ass down shit we need them bricks or something ♪

I was feeling optimistic about this big change in my life as Jada and I filled, taped and marked boxes inside of my room while the surround sound was bumpin' Chief Keef.

I attempted to dance the jitters of the move away as I wrapped my purses in tissue paper. "*Keep this shit one hunna. I keep this shit three hunna. I pull up in that Audi. You pull up in that Honda...*" I was rapping along to the lyrics until I caught a glimpse of Jada staring at me with her lip poked out. "What's wrong?"

"I can't fucking believe this." Jada's lip was poked out like a kid as she placed my shoes in a box while sitting in the middle of the closet. She wouldn't even look me in my face, though. I know that she felt my eyes on her, while I stood behind her packing my purses. "I can't believe you're really moving."

I sighed. Though Jada was four years older than me, we had grown so close, especially since King and I got together. Instead of "cousins," we often called each other "sister-baby mama-cousin-friend," because we played all of those roles in each other's lives. We had grown from cousins to best friends to damn near sisters and were like mothers to one another's children. "I know. I can't believe it either. A part of me doesn't want to even go."

"Then why are you goiiing?" she whined.

"I just want to follow my dreams, Jada," I pouted.

"I know," she admitted. "You know I want you to go down to Atlanta and become that doctor. Then maybe you can prescribe something to my crazy ass kids." We both giggled as she continued. "It's just...I'm going to miss y'all. You're my cousin and my friend, and King is like a brother to me. King, Meech, and Dolla have been running together a long time, and, even though the partnership is not breaking up, it's going to be hard to see them apart."

When King told me that he would actually move to Atlanta with me and Kayla, I believed him, but it felt unreal. He was willing to leave everything he'd built and everyone he loved to be with me. But then he actually bought the house in Atlanta, and we started to prepare to move. It was suddenly real for the entire crew, and seeing everyone's sadness made me feel so much guilt.

But I appreciated King's sacrifice, and it made me love him that much more.

"I'm sorry," was all that I could say as I knelt behind her and wrapped my arms around her.

"Don't be, girl. You got a good man, and he is doing this for you. Don't be sorry. Be proud." She didn't even sound like she believed those words herself, but she was being a friend and supporting me like always. "Plus, now I have a reason to sneak down to the A! I heard the strip clubs be poppin' down there!"

"You've never been to Atlanta?"

"Nope. Never. Never been anywhere. The only trips that I've taken are the road trips I go on for the crew," she admitted sadly. "And that's to boring ass places like Idaho, Maryland, and Ohio."

"Damn! Really? You and Dolla need to go on a vacation."

"Well, if his ass ever marries me, maybe we can go somewhere like Jamaica or Mexico for our honeymoon." The smile on her face was so surreal as if she could smell the fresh water and feel the sand between her toes. "Yeah, that'll be dope."

"Why haven't you and Dolla gotten married yet?"

"Because we were so young when we got together that, though we were having kids, we felt like we were too young for marriage. Then he was cheating and shit, so I didn't want to marry him. Then he got to that stage that most niggas get to when they are scared to get married, like a bitch gon' leave him and take him for everything he got... which a bitch would, if he tried to leave me!" We giggled as she continued, and I gave her a high five. "But now he is finally maturing, and with the business going as good as it is, he can focus more on family, so I'm sure it's coming."

"I'm sure it is too, cousin." Then the cutest idea hit me. "Oooo! What if it's soon? Then we can have a double wedding. All four of us can go to Cabo together!"

"Is that where King is taking you for your honeymoon?"

I grinned at the thought of it. "Yeah."

"That's dope. If the four of us could all go, that would be really dope! But we can't leave Meech and Siren out."

I sucked my teeth, saying, "Siren probably wouldn't even want to go."

"I know, right? I don't know what's been up with her lately."

For the past few months, Siren had been real stank. She didn't want to hang out, and she was not answering our calls as much. She was avoiding the crew altogether.

"I'ma get on her ass during this run tonight, though. We gon' be in the car for a whole day together, so she ain't gon' have no choice but to hear me out and tell me what the fuck her problem is."

"And as soon as she tells you, call me and tell me!"

Now she was giving me a high five. "I shol' will!" Then she returned to the box that she was taping while asking, "Anyway, when are you and King going to tie the knot?"

"In two more years, when I graduate with my bachelor's."

"Are you going to stay in Atlanta to get your master's too?"

"I don't know. I want to see how we adjust to this move before I even start thinking about that."

Jada nodded in agreement as I heard King calling my name. "Kennedy! Babe, come here!"

"I'll be back, girl," I told Jada as I jogged out of the room and down the stairs while I followed King's voice. He had been gone all day and hadn't been answering the phone, so I figured something was up, and I was anxious to see what.

"Hey, baby." I greeted him with a kiss as we met at the bottom of the stairs. When he barely kissed me back, I got nervous. Then when he held both of my hands, I got scared as shit. "What's wrong?"

"Nothing is wrong, I just..." His eyes found the floor. "I have to go make a run tonight."

"Why *you*?"

"Dolla and Meech are tailing Siren and Jada tonight. It's a big shipment and the buyer only wants to fuck with Meech and Dolla when it gets there. It's really nobody else that I can trust to do this shit, and it has to be done tonight. My guy got robbed the other night, and he needs to re-up bad to get his money up. He wants ten bricks, and I ain't tryin' to lose out on no money." I didn't like the look in King's eyes. He was uncomfortable and nervous. He made deals and money, not drops. I didn't want him on the road. All I imagined was him being pulled over, and my entire life being snatched from up under me. King in the driver's seat on the freeway was like a waving flag beckoning the police to pull him over.

"Where are you going?" I asked.

"Just to Indianapolis. I'm going to leave tonight and shoot right back in the morning."

I bit my lips anxiously. I didn't feel right about King being out there like a sitting duck. "I'll go."

King's eyes bucked. "What? Hell nah!"

"No, seriously, King. I'll go. I'd rather go than risk a chance of you being stopped."

I knew that he agreed with me because his anxiety went away as soon as I said it, but still there was so much reluctance in his eyes. "I'll tail you then."

"Then who is going to be here with Kayla? My mother is working midnights." As he continued to ponder, I continued to convince him. "It's cool. You said this is one of your friends, right?'

"Yeah," he answered slowly.

"Then you won't have anything to worry about. I won't need anyone with me. Just tell him that you're sending your girl."

He was still reluctant, and it was kind of irritating. They trusted Jada and Siren with these things, but King always kept me caged up like a bird. King had done a lot for me. He had made so many sacrifices, so something in me just wanted to do something for him for once. "I can do it, King. It can't be that hard. You're asking for trouble by hitting that road yourself. I can't take you being locked up. I need you, especially to pay my fucking tuition."

As he giggled, he let his guard down and kissed my forehead. "A'ight. I guess it's cool. You're right. He is my friend, so he'll be cool with making the transaction with you."

"Cool. Just don't tell, Jada. She'll be so mad that I'm doing this. She protects me more than you do."

He winked and kissed me softly before saying, "Your secret is safe with me, baby girl."

****

♪You can look me in my face
I ain't got no worries
I ain't got no worries
I ain't got no worries
See the sh-rooms keep me up
I ain't got no worries
I ain't got no worries
I ain't got no worries ♪

I was cruising down 94 East clutching the wheel with one hand and a cup of coffee in the other to keep me awake. I was bobbing my head to Lil' Wayne as King spoke to me through my Bluetooth earpiece.

"King, you don't have to talk to me for the entire ride."

"Yes, I do."

I sucked my teeth with a smile. "You don't talk to Siren and Jada the entire time."

"Nah, I don't. But they aren't my fiancée, and they didn't have my baby. You are, and you did, so I'm talking to you until you get to Indianapolis."

I shook my head, rebutting only in silence. There was no use in saying anything. King was going to do exactly whatever the hell he wanted to do. Besides, I had been on the road for only thirty minutes and had three more hours to go. I was positive that someone was going to call him soon with important business, and he'd be forced to leave me the hell alone.

There wasn't much to focus on, though. For a Monday evening, the highway was practically empty. I was pushing the black 2011 Jeep Cherokee at an easy fifty-five miles per hour, only five miles over the speed limit. As I listened to King talk to me about details of the move, I imagined that, to anyone passing me, I looked like any other college student that used this highway to get back and forth from school to home. No one would be able to look at that jeep and assume that I was riding with over two hundred thousand dollars of the purest cocaine available in the Midwest.

That's what I had assumed, at least. The crew had made this run many, many times before without any issues. Siren and Jada had made so many runs over the years that they would be indicted for the rest of their lives if the Feds knew, but they had never been stopped for even a fucking traffic violation.

"I can't wait either. That pool is so amazing. I can't wait to get Kayla in there." I was smiling and imagining playing with Kayla in the in-ground pool in the backyard of our new house down south. I could imagine the constant warm weather as I went from class to class while King and Kayla waited for me back at home. I could not wait for this dream to finally come true.

"Hell nah," I heard King fuss. "I don't want my baby girl in no damn pool."

I started cracking up. "Just because you're scared to swim don't mean–"

Red and blue lights in the rearview mirror stopped me.

"Hello? Kennedy?" I heard King calling out to me.

"Shit," I breathed.

"What's wrong?!"

"Fuck! Fuck! Fuck!" I was freaking out as I pulled over. I was hoping that they were pulling over somebody else, but as I pulled over to the shoulder, so did the squad car. They were definitely stopping me.

"Kennedy?" I could hear King frantically shouting in my ear. "Kennedy!"

I felt so stupid. Out of everything that he had done for me, the one thing that I had done for him, I had managed to fuck it up.

But maybe not. *Calm down, Kennedy. Just calm down*, I silently told myself.

"Hello?"

Maybe they are just stopping me for speeding or something. But I wasn't speeding.

"Kennedy!"

Finally, I snapped out of it and responded. "I'm getting pulled over."

"What? Were you speeding?"

"I was just going fifty-five."

"Just be cool, baby. Maybe it's just some bullshit moving violation."

But as I saw two police officers approaching the car with their hands defensively on their guns, I knew that it was far from a bullshit moving violation. My gut was telling me that something was about to go very wrong, and I instantly felt so much guilt for fucking up.

I watched them through the side mirror. One went to the passenger side, and the other tapped my driver's side window. He peered down into the car, using a flashlight that was blinding me.

"Kennedy, what's happening?" I could hear King ask me as the police officer tapped on the window again with his gun with so much force that, even though I watched him and was expecting it, I jumped.

"Kennedy?!" King shouted into my ear.

"I gotta go King."

"No, don't hang–"

I had hung up on him in midsentence, not even on purpose. I wasn't thinking. My mind was so cloudy as I tried to focus on not fucking up any further. I had to get back home to King and Kayla. It was imperative, just as important as my next breath.

I could see that King was calling right back just as soon as I started to roll the window down. I hoped that I would be able to call him back as soon as they took my license, registration, and insurance and went back to the car to do whatever it was that they do that took them fifteen minutes before they finally returned with your ticket.

But that is far from what happened. As soon as I rolled the window down, he aimed his gun and ordered, "Step out of the vehicle." He even pulled on the door handle, as if he would be able to open it without me unlocking the door.

I through my hands up. "Okay, okay," I told him as his partner's flashlight illuminated the inside of the car. "I'm unlocking the door." With one hand, I unlocked the door slowly while keeping the other hand in the air, in sight. I then got out of the car with my heart beating at one hundred miles an hour. I was freaking out, but trying desperately not to show it. Before long, the officer returned his gun to the holster with one hand and grabbed me with the other.

"What's going on? Why are you stopping me?"

He didn't say anything as he cuffed my wrists. "Step into the squad car, ma'am. We have probable cause to search the vehicle."

Scared was an understatement. Disappointed in myself was a definite. I didn't know much about the law because I hadn't been stopped for as much as a traffic ticket. Though I hadn't been read my Miranda rights, as they began to search the car, I knew the night was not going to end well.

KING

Each minute that went by felt like an eternity and every hour that went by, I experienced a new death.

"King, c'mon. You gotta calm down. We gotta figure this shit out."

I could hear Meech, but that shit was going in one ear and out the other. My head was down on the kitchen table as I tried to keep down the contents of my stomach. I was sick–*literally*.

It had been four hours since I talked to Kennedy…four hours since I'd heard her voice. I knew what that meant. She had been arrested, and they were questioning the shit out of her before allowing her to make a phone call.

"I called the jail out there," Jada stated. "They got her." As soon as I heard the words, breath left my body. With my head on the kitchen table, my leg bounced up and down frantically. I was trying to figure out how the fuck this happened. We had done this so many times that it could have been done in our sleep. Now my baby was being held, and I couldn't even help her. That shit made me feel helpless, and I didn't like that weak ass shit.

"We gotta go, King." Jada was right. That's what we should have been doing, and I was glad that they had turned around and come right back home when they got the call that Kennedy had been arrested. If they hadn't been there, I wouldn't have been able to do that shit alone.

When I finally lifted my head, I knew that I looked pathetic because Jada, Meech, Dolla and Siren looked at me with so much sympathy. Their sympathy was confirmation that this shit was truly fucked up.

"King, man..." Dolla started, trying to find the right words to say. "Maybe they didn't find shit."

"They found something, man. They arrested her. What the fuck else was in the car for them to arrest her for?" Anger took over. I smacked the expensive table settings that Kennedy loved off of the table, causing them to go flying into the air and against the wall.

Everyone except Siren was too scared to approach me. "King, you gotta get your shit together and go get your girl. Meech is calling the lawyer so that he can go up there to see what's going on. Yeah, this shit is fucked up, but you can cry about this shit tomorrow. Right now, we have moves to make. Let's go." We hadn't spoken in months, since I broke her heart in the hospital the day that Kayla was born, but she was still the one that knew me better than them all.

Just then, Jada appeared in the doorway of the kitchen. She had Kayla wrapped in her pink Baby Phat blanket and was carrying the baby bag over her shoulder. I had forgotten all about Kayla in the midst of the chaos. Looking at the top of her curly fro, I broke. Tears that I had fought back, because of the presence of my homies, rose to the surface. Our family was about to split up.

It didn't matter that we had lost damn near half a million on two unsuccessful deliveries that night. Kayla and Kennedy's future was worth more than all that shit, and I had just fucked that all up because I let Kennedy convince me to allow her to make that run.

"C'mon, bro," Dolla said, bringing me back to this fucked up reality. "Let's ride."

The mood was eerie as we all slunk out of the house with solemn looks on our faces. I hated that shit. We had never had this among our crew. We were experiencing sadness and regret. Any time that we had an issue, we handled that shit. We had killed snitches and thieves so swiftly that issues had become few and far between because foes feared the shit out of us. But in this situation there was no one to kill in order to make these charges go away, but myself. Being away from my family and my crew was a suicide mission that I was about to have to take.

During the ride to the county, I wondered how this could've happened. The police had to have been tipped off. But by who? There was no telling. The possibilities were endless. For all I knew, my nigga in Indianapolis had set me up. Or Reese was in prison talking to get out or lighten his sentence. Maybe the Feds weren't really done when they arrested Reese, and they had been watching us all along.

KENNEDY

It was proving to be the longest night of my life. Not even when I gave birth to Kayla had I cried so much or felt so much pain.

As I sat in the back of the squad car, I prayed that this was just a random search. But as the officer climbed out of the backseat of the Jeep holding rectangle-shaped objects wrapped in brown paper, I knew that this shit was far from random.

How did they know where the stash spot was?

More squad cars came, and then detectives. Cars slowly drove by the scene, peering into the window and gaping at me. I felt like such a fucking failure. I thought of Kayla and Spelman and felt like a fucking fool. Not once did I feel stupid for making the run, I just felt dumb for failing King and my baby girl.

All the while, King's voice rang in my head. The words that he'd told me the day that he asked me to officially be his woman played over and over again in my head like a sad love song. *I do a lot of shit that will send me away forever if I ever get caught.*

Two hours later, I was being thrown into a small room with dirty, tan walls. I sat there for God only knew how long. Out of the window, I could hear crickets and smell the night air. I imagined that it was at least after midnight by then.

I had worn myself out from crying so long and so hard. Sounds of the old wooden door opening brought me out of my sleep. I swear, even as I woke up, I had to remember where I was and why. And as the badges of the detectives came into view, the realization was numbing.

"Hi, Miss Mitchell. I'm Detective Sanchez," the Latina detective started, as she sat at the table across from me. "Let's just get straight to the point. There were a lot of drugs in your car... a *whole lot*. I've run a background check on you. You have no criminal record. You're in college. I saw your school ID in your purse. Who were you running these drugs for? Just tell us his name and where to find him, and this will all go away."

Him. That's all that I heard. *How do they know?*

She reached over and held my hand. I looked into her eyes as frightened tears streamed down my face. Her eyes were so kind. She wasn't that old, but she had caring eyes like my mother.

"Baby girl, don't ruin your future like this. Just tell us so that we can get you out of here and back home where you belong."

She was right; I belonged back home with my family, but King had never ever turned his back on me, and I wasn't about to turn my back on him. "I want a lawyer."

With that, she sucked her teeth and gave me a look of sympathy. She knew that I was taking this for someone else, and her judgmental eyes told me that she knew exactly for who. She felt like I was being a dumb woman for a nigga that probably wasn't shit anyway. But if she only knew; it was the exact opposite. King had loved me to the point that he deserved my loyalty, even when I was facing my own demise.

I was being charged with possession of a controlled substance, a felony charge that carried a max of ten years because of how much drugs it was. As I sat in the cell all night, I couldn't sleep. I just kept thinking about how my future was about to change for the worse. I was worried about myself but, most of all, about King. I knew that he was worried sick, but I got sicker as I thought of having to face him after this.

They were taking forever to allow me to make a phone call, and I was about to give up being able to call anyone until a police officer showed up in front of my cell.

"You have a visitor."

For once in the past few hours, I felt relief. I didn't know who the fuck it was, but I was relieved to be able to talk to somebody. But once I was led out of the cell and into the visitation area, I stared oddly at the older, white guy in the grey suit. He was sitting on the other side of the glass, holding a phone, and staring at me with a smile.

Once I put the phone to my ear, he identified himself. "Hi. I'm David Thomas," he told me. "I'm your lawyer."

My eyebrows curled with question. "Who hired you?"

"King."

At the sound of his name, I let out a deep sigh and began to sob. Strangely enough, I wasn't crying because of my fate. I was crying because I had let him down. I had let the entire crew down.

"Kennedy, calm down," Mr. Thomas urged through the thick glass. "Listen to me. We are going to get you out of here in the morning, okay?" I was too overcome to even face him; all I could do was cry as I hid my face in my hands. "King and all of your friends are outside. They can't come in, but King wanted me to tell you that he loves you and that he's sorry." I was sobbing uncontrollably at that point. Moans and wails left my throat, mirroring enduring pain.

SEPTEMBER 2012

CHAPTER EIGHTEEN

KENNEDY

With my record and education, the judge figured that I had just been caught up with the wrong man. The next morning during my hearing, I was given a bail that Jada had paid on behalf of King, who was outside of the county waiting for me. As I was being processed, Mr. Thomas informed me that the prosecutors were expecting me to turn over the name of the person that the drugs belonged to in exchange for the charges to be dropped. They figured that a ten-year sentence would scare a young mother of nineteen that was in college into cooperating.

But even a month after my arrest, I was still totally against snitching on King.

"Luckily, you didn't make it across state lines. Otherwise, this would be a federal case." Mr. Thomas paused and took a deep breath. "You have two choices here. You can give up King, so your charges can be dropped–"

"I'm not giving them anything," I told Mr. Thomas as King and I sat across from him in his office.

I could hear King already sighing in protest. "Kenne–"

I rolled my eyes and tried not to fuss with the love of my life. "What's the other option?" I asked Mr. Thomas. "What are they offering?"

"If you plead guilty, they're offering eight years. You'd have to serve four."

"She's not serving shit," King cut in. "She'll give me up."

"I'm not doing it, King," I argued.

"Kennedy, baby," he said with a grimace on his face. I knew he was trying hard to keep his composure, but my rebuttal was pissing him off more and more. "This ain't no movie, babe. This ain't Bonnie and Clyde, and you ain't got to prove shit to me." There was so much urgency in his voice. He was literally begging me. "I can't have my woman sitting in no fucking prison because of me. That shit go against everything I stand for. What about Kayla?"

"What about me, King? What about me living without you for the rest of my life because I turned you in? I can't live with that!"

"It won't be for the rest of my life, bae."

I turned to Mr. Thomas, who was looking at us with empathy. "How much time can he get if I give him up, Mr. Thomas?" King raised his hand at Mr. Thomas, signaling for him not to answer me, but I insisted. "He's paying you, but you are *my* lawyer! How much time can he get?"

He sighed deeply. "I'm sure they already have pending investigations on him, and with the previous convictions on his record, that will only blow the case wide open. He would be looking at thirty years at least."

I looked at King like he was crazy. "And you want me to do that to you? I'm offended as fuck that you would even expect me to do that!"

"And I'm offended that you would expect me to go out like some punk ass bitch!"

"Fuck your pride, King! What about all these people out here that are depending on you to eat? What about Meech? What about Dolla? Huh?! What about their kids? Why risk all of their lives when I can just take this deal and—"

"No!" King's hand smacked against the table so hard that Mr. Thomas and I jumped out of our skin, and it threatened to shatter. Even Kayla moved in her sleep as she sat in her stroller near the door of the office. "I said no, gawd damn it!" I saw the tears forming in King's eyes, so I knew to just shut the fuck up. I had never seen him weep before I was arrested, but for a month he had literally been weeping. He felt so guilty that he was physically sick. He had not been eating, and he'd barely been sleeping. "*I said no*," he insisted through a clenched jaw, now a bit calmer as he wiped his eyes. "You're not taking no fucking deal, Kennedy.

You're not ruining your life. You're going to be here for Kayla. You're going to move to Atlanta, and you're going to go to Spelman. That's what the fuck is going to happen. You hear me?"

I nodded as I swallowed the lump in my throat. "Okay."

"You hear me?" he asked again, staring me deep in the eyes.

"Yes, I hear you."

King took a deep breath, relieved that I was finally seeing things his way. He looked at Mr. Thomas, and, I swear, Mr. Thomas was looking at him doubtfully, silently asking him if he was sure if this was truly what he wanted to do. But King ignored him. "So what happens now?"

Mr. Thomas cleared the lump his throat. "We'll meet with the prosecutor during her court appearance Friday and discuss terms of her cooperation with the State, and then we'll go from there."

King nodded, and with that, his fate was sealed.

King

"Can we get married?"

I looked at Kennedy as she sat in the front seat. Her eyes were puffy as tears pooled at the surface of them. I felt her pain. I wanted to cry too, but a nigga had shed so many tears lately that I was starting to question my manhood.

"We are getting married, baby," I told her as I put the key in the ignition. "This case ain't stopping shit. I'm sure they gon' try to offer me a deal, but I ain't takin' that shit. Trials can take years, so we have time to get married, baby."

"No, King," she told me as she laid her hand on my thigh. "I mean, can we get married today?"

I let go of the key right before turning the engine on and sat back in the driver's seat, just staring at Kennedy, wondering if she was serious, but the tears streaming down her face testified to her truth and genuineness.

I reached over and held her hand. "Why?"

And she actually forced a smile through her tears. "You don't want to marry me anymore?"

There had been so many moments that showed me why Kennedy was my queen, but since she was arrested, those reasons were shoved into my face. She was a true rider. She showed me the true definition of unconditional love. Even during our darkest moments, even with tears stressing her beautiful smile, as she sat there in a flowing green sundress and ponytail, she was the true definition of love and beauty. No one had taught me what that was. Not my mother, nor a father that I never knew. But, unbeknownst to her, she had taught me that. That was why I had to protect her. No matter what it meant for me, I could never let her go down for this.

"Of course, I do."

"Then let's go get married," she insisted as she leaned over, exposing her breasts and putting her lips so close to mine that I could smell the flavor of her lips gloss. "Right now. We're already downtown."

"I thought you wanted a big wedding? I thought you wanted to wait?"

Her eyes saddened. "We can't do that if you're going to be gone."

"You never know what will happen, bae. Mr. Thomas can work wonders. I might not get as much time as we think."

"But I don't want anything else to happen to eith–"

"Nothing else is going to happen–"

"If...*If* anything else happens, I don't want it to without me being Mrs. Carter."

Even in the most stressful state of our relationship, she could still have anything she wanted. "Okay," I answered as I finally turned the engine. "Whatever you want, baby. Let's go."

So we headed to the courthouse to get married.

KENNEDY

"Damn, Mrs. Carter," King breathed into my ear. "Fuck!"

I smiled at the sound of his deep voice breathing desire and hunger into my ear. I began to play along his neck with my tongue as my fingers played with his locs.

"I fucking love this pussy." He said that like he was mad that he loved it so much.

"She loves you too, baby."

We had told one another that we loved each other so many times since the day that we got married. Only me, King, and Kayla were present. And although she whimpered and cried the entire time, our courthouse wedding was beautiful to me and a day that I would never forget. We were both simply dressed, me in a sundress and he in jeans and a tee. I even had on flips flops. His locs needed to be restyled, and his roots needed to be twisted. My hair was in a ponytail. There was no beautiful, mouth-dropping white dress as I had fantasized about. There was no charming, white, Gucci suit that I had imagined him in. There was no altar and no flowers. It was just me, the man that I planned to love for the rest of my life, and our daughter.

It was perfect.

That was four days ago. We had spent the following days together, literally. It had been me, King and Kayla at dinner or in the house laid up with one another. We were enjoying our marital bliss while getting adjusted to the fact that soon King would be going away for a very long time. He didn't know when exactly he would be going. We figured that once I appeared in court that Friday and spoke to the prosecutor, a warrant would be issued for his arrest. So he had spent every single day between then loving on me and Kayla. He hadn't even hung out with Dolla and Meech, who he had told what the plan was. Obviously, everyone was very heartbroken that King, *our king*, would be gone possibly for the rest of our lives, but they all respected his decision.

"Shit!" King cursed through heavy gasps. "I swear I'm gon' miss this pussy the most."

I felt his dick hardening like concrete between my walls. I knew that he was then cumming, so I lifted my legs to allow him to sink deeper into my wetness. "Shit!" he cursed again, his rhythm quickening to a fast, steady place. "Gawd damn," he groaned through gritted teeth.

"That's it, King. I love this dick so much. Cum on, baby. Cum in my pussy."

That was all it took. King was gripping my waist for dear life with his neck buried in my neck as his love burst inside of me.

We laid there for a few moments, sweating, breathing hard, and holding each other. This time in our relationship was so bittersweet. We were more in love than we had ever been because we knew that we were about to be apart for a very long time.

"I have to get ready for court," I said regretfully. "Jada and Siren should be here in a minute."

It was Friday; doomsday.

King sighed deeply but didn't move.

"King–"

"I don't want you to go."

Again, my hands ran through his locs lovingly. "I know. Me either. But I have to."

He sighed once more as he rolled over and off of me.

"You'll be here when I get back, right?"

King looked at me like I was crazy. "Of course."

Though he was expecting for the warrant to be issued for his arrest, King had never and would never voluntarily go to the county, so he was not coming to court with me. It wasn't smart for him or his business. He needed to stay under the radar until the police were forced to come under it and find him.

I sighed again and smiled at him before kissing him quickly and getting out of the bed to shower. If I hadn't gotten up then, I would have never had the nerve to get up and do what I had to do.

An hour and a half later, I was walking toward the county building with Jada and Siren. I could see my mother standing with Mr. Thomas.

Surprisingly, my mother had been very supportive since my arrest. Since she was from the streets, she knew how shit like this could happen. She pitied me instead of faulting me and was there for me every step of the way. She was so unlike my father, who we never even bothered to tell what was happening.

Walking into the courthouse felt like I was walking the Green Mile, like I was walking to my death. But for once since the cops had pulled me over, I felt confident that this was what needed to be done.

Mr. Thomas spoke to me outside of the courtroom for a few minutes, going over the plan. The plan was for him to tell the prosecutor that I would give them all the information on King, in exchange for the charges being dropped against me. Once inside of the courtroom, I saw him having a conversation with the prosecutor. Jada and my mom held my hand, calming me down, smoothing away my tears, and Siren continued to give me supportive smiles. Though they were supporting me, I could see the despair in their faces for King.

"Case number 1237. The State of Illinois versus Kennedy Desiree King."

I stood and met Mr. Thomas at the defendant's table with wobbly knees.

The judge eyed me, seemingly surprised at the short, round girl wearing a black, midi, sheath dress, flats, reading glasses and a mere ponytail.

"Prosecution, go ahead," the judge ordered.

"Your Honor, I've spoken with Mr. Thomas regarding Mrs. Carter agreeing to cooperate with the state in exchange for the charges to be dropped."

The judge looked at me above his glasses asking, "Mrs. Carter, is that true? Do you agree with these terms?"

"No," I immediately said, and as soon as the word left my mouth I heard gasps from Jada, Siren, and my mother. Mr. Thomas instantly swung around and stared at me with bulging eyes. "I'd like to plead guilty, Your Honor. I'd like to take the deal that was offered to me if it's still on the table."

I couldn't face Mr. Thomas. I knew that he was pissed. But I could see him staring at the side of my face. "Excuse me, Your Honor. Please give me a moment with my client."

"Sure, Mr. Thomas," he agreed as he sat back in his big leather chair.

Mr. Thomas raised his manila folder to hide our conversation. "What are you doing, Kennedy?" he frantically whispered.

I looked at him like the shit was obvious. "I'm pleading guilty."

"King said–"

My eyes rolled back into my head. "I don't care what King said. You're my lawyer, and I want to plead guilty."

As we held a stare for a few seconds, I could hear harsh whispers from Jada behind me. "Kennedy! Kennedy!"

Mr. Thomas continued to stare at me, so I insisted, "I'm pleading guilty. That's it."

"They can take the deal off of the table now. They are going to be pissed. They want King."

My hand went to my hips. Though I had been sure for a long time, my heart was beating like a beast, realizing that I was really about to go to prison. I was about to be away from my baby and King, but I continued to remind myself that it was for the best. "I'm pleading guilty. Don't make me say it again."

With a deep breath, Mr. Thomas turned back toward the judge. "Your Honor, my client would like to plead guilty."

"Kennedy!" I couldn't even turn toward Jada while the judge banged his gavel as she continued. "Kennedy, what the fuck are you doing?"

Tears came to my eyes as I heard the desperation in her voice. My heart ached, and the tears began to flow as I imagined the pain that my mother was feeling.

"Bailiff, remove that young lady from the courtroom!" the judge ordered.

I lowered my head as I heard feet shuffling against the floor of the courtroom.

"Kennedy, no! What the fuck?" I still couldn't turn to face Jada, but her voice was becoming more and more faint. And then I could hear the big door of the courtroom open and then close.

The judge frustratingly ran his fingers through his gray hair as he adjusted his glasses and skimmed papers that were in front of him. "Mrs. Carter, are you sure about your plea?"

"Yes, Your Honor," I answered with shaky breath.

He looked at the prosecutor. "Is the plea deal still on the table?"

Even the prosecutor was taken aback by my sudden change of heart. "Your Honor," the prosecutor started. "We...um..."

But it wasn't a change of heart. I had never intended to turn King in. I couldn't send my man to prison and live with myself. Even as he yelled in Mr. Thomas' office that day, I knew what I was going to do. That is why I wanted to get married that day, so that when I did this, I would at least be King's wife. "Yes, we'll honor the deal." I could hear the defeat all in her voice. "Eight years in exchange for a guilty plea."

"Yes, I read it." Then the judge took a deep sigh. I knew from conversations with Mr. Thomas that the judge had the choice to accept the deal or sentence me to a longer term. My heart beat wildly, waiting for my fate. But seconds later, he finally said, "So ordered. The defendant is to serve a term of eight years," the judge commanded. "The defendant will turn herself in on November 10th."

****

After I signed the deal, with shaking hands and sweaty palms, my fate was sealed, and King was still free. He was still free to take care of all of us. Despite my own fate, I was happy with King's. As

I walked out of the courtroom, with Mr. Thomas following me, I knew that I had made a decision out of love, not stupidity.

But Jada didn't feel that way. "What the fuck, Kennedy?! What did you do?!"

I looked up to see her charging toward me with tears streaming down her face. Many people, who were coming and going from the courthouse, looked at us. As she walked toward me, I walked past her. I needed to get her as far away from that courthouse as fast as possible because I didn't need her arrested next for disorderly conduct.

I could hear her following closely behind me, crying. She was on my heels as I walked past my crying mother and a somber Siren.

"Kennedy, I can't believe you!" She was pulling on my arm as she screeched at me. "Why would you do that?"

Now that we were finally on the side of the courthouse, I spun around. "You expected me to turn on my nigga? Did you really expect me to do that?" Jada's face finally transformed from anger to sympathy because her tears met mine. "I'm sorry, but I wasn't about to do that shit. He loves me. He adores me. I don't need for shit. I ain't never caught him with a bitch. He ain't never turned on me, so I ain't turning on him!"

Jada just cried and shook her head. My mother approached me, wrapped her arms around my waist and laid her head on my shoulder. Siren comforted Jada, who seemed to be taking it worse than I was.

"Jada, if King would have gone away, this shit would have been over. And you might as well have buried me because I would have died, so you would have been crying either way. Jada..." I paused with a sigh. "Now everybody can keep living, and I'll be back."

She looked at me, ready to say something. Her tear soaked lips parted, and just as she was about to speak, tires screeching took our attention away from one another. We looked toward the car that was approaching us.

Fuck, I thought with a sigh just as my mother said, "Oh God."

King's Camaro was damn near on the curb. In all of the chaos, I had totally forgotten about facing him. We had never lied to each other. We had never been disloyal. And as he jumped out of the driver's side with the car still running, I could see the shock and hurt in his eyes as he barged toward me.

"Take your ass in there and tell them that you take that shit back!" His presence was already scary, but with the current chilling look on his face and glare in his eyes, he was a beast. My mother stood at my side, stiff with fear and sympathy, and I was barely able to look at him.

"Go take it back!" He was in my face with spit spraying from his lips. I could see anger in his eyes, but I also saw the pain in his heart.

"I can't," I cried. "I'm sorry, King, but I can't."

"She signed the deal, King," I heard Mr. Thomas say behind me.

King looked at me with disappointment, so much disappointment that I had never seen meant for me. That hurt the worst of all, but I knew that, once he calmed down, he would remember that I was still that smart, ambitious, loving girl that he fell in love with that would never be so stupid as to turn her back on her man.

"Mr. Thomas, can't you holla at them?" The heart-wrenching sound of his voice was tragic for all of us. We all looked on in pity. Tears were in all of our eyes as we watched King beg for my freedom with a painful wince in his voice. "Can't you fix this shit, man?"

Mr. Thomas' jaws tightened with regret. "I'm sorry, King. It's final."

King swung around and looked at me like he didn't know who I was anymore. "Fuck!"

He kicked a bottle on the ground, and it went flying through the air and hit a parked squad car.

"King!" Siren shouted. "You gotta calm down!"

"Come on, y'all," Jada said with a sigh. "Let's go. Let's get out of here." When Jada went to grab King, he violently snatched his arm away from her with so much force that she flinched.

But my mother was able to calm him down as she stood in front of him staring him down with a motherly glare. "King, I know you're upset. But she loves you. What did you think she would do?" King bit his lip. I could imagine that he was fighting whatever disrespectful words that wanted to spew from his mouth, fighting them back because he respected my mother. "She is the same intelligent girl that you married. The same strong girl that you told me that you admire. This was a smart move she just made, and it was a strong move. And it was love, King. It was a move that she made out of *love*." My heart broke as the sun shined on King's tears as they slid from his tightly closed eyes. "Don't you do this," my mother continued. "Don't you punish her for loving you *this* much."

A small, deep moan left King's throat as he opened his eyes and looked at me. He was so big and his arms were so long that he was able to reach past my mother for me.

"I'm sorry," I cried as he pulled me into his chest and wrapped his arms around me. "I'm sorry, baby, but I just couldn't do it."

"I know, baby. I know," he insisted as he kissed the top of my head. "I'm sorry too."

SIREN

Oh hell naw!

"Unt uh!" My walk sped up as soon as I saw that bitch. "Get the hell away from me!"

It was amazing how this heffa seemed to find me everywhere I went.

"Now, now, Siren." Her voice was so irritating that it made my skin crawl. What was worse was that the bitch had the nerve to grab me by my elbow as I was unlocking my car door. She was lucky she was the damn police. Otherwise, I would have whooped her ass.

I sucked my teeth as I turned around to face her. "Why would you do that? That's not what you said you were going to do! Kennedy ain't got no business going to jail! You were supposed to arrest King, not her!"

Detective Sanchez looked around the parking lot of the Harold's that we were standing next to. I had just left out of there, hurriedly on my way back home to feed Meech and Elijah. I didn't feel like cooking after leaving King's house, and Meech barely felt like eating, to be honest. We were all just so fucked up about what was happening with Kennedy, and watching King suffer was tragic. I loved him so much, and he had hurt me, but he was so sick over Kennedy's sentencing that even I felt bad for him. I especially felt bad because it was my fault.

Detective Sanchez noticed a few people staring at us, so she pulled me toward the other end of the parking lot near the alley where her unmarked car was parked. She was in plain clothes, but anybody would wonder what this older, Latino lady was doing in the hood. Still I walked with reluctance. I wanted nothing to do with this bitch from the moment I met her a few months ago.

I was so pissed when I left the hospital the day that King proposed to Kayla that I went back into the room, told Meech that I wasn't feeling well and got the hell up out of there. I was speeding through the city while listening to every sad, love song you could think of, not even paying attention to my surroundings. I was totally caught off guard when I got pulled over by an unmarked detective's car. I couldn't imagine why they would be interested in writing a speeding ticket; that is, until Detective Sanchez came to the window asking me what I was doing driving around in the car owned by Demetrius Stewart, known in the streets as Meech. I didn't say a word, and that only pissed her off, so she snatched me out of Meech's car and threw me in the back of hers while she searched his. I wasn't surprised when she found the drugs and guns in the trunk. I had been on my way to drop them off at the trap for Meech when Kennedy went into labor.

What did surprise me was when she came back to the car and told me, "There are two things that can happen now. I can arrest you and send you away for a very long time, or you can help me put King away."

I was shocked. King had never been on the radar of the Feds or the state authorities. He was squeaky clean, but apparently through wiretaps of another supplier she had come across King's name. Detective Sanchez was a narcotics detective who had been investigating King for months, which was how she ended up stopping me as I left the hospital. So far she had been coming up with nothing. There was absolutely no substantial evidence against King, or Dolla and Meech for that matter, that would stand up in court. She was hoping that it was Meech in the car as she pulled me over so that she could get him to cooperate. To her dismay, it was only me, but little did she know, I had it out for King just like she did.

When I told her, "That's cool," so quickly, her eyes bulged in shock, but she was pleased.

Leaving that hospital, I wanted nothing more but to see King suffer as much as I was. Detective Sanchez was right on time. But still I had battled with if I should really do the shit or not. King had hurt me, and he was a thoughtless son of a bitch for how he had treated me over the years. It would have made me feel a hundred times better if he'd just gone away. So finally, when I heard that he was actually moving to Atlanta with that nerd bitch, I got the courage. I wanted to teach King a lesson and ensure that Kennedy wasn't able to fly down to Atlanta and live my happily ever after. Meech gave me the perfect opportunity when he left the patio door open as he was on the phone with King discussing the run that King had to make to Indianapolis that night. Jada and I were driving one of the two cars that they used to make runs, so I knew the exact make, model and plate number to give Detective Sanchez when I discreetly called her from the bathroom.

I stood near the alley of the parking lot glaring at Detective Sanchez as she giggled.

"This shit ain't funny! That girl is going to jail, and it's all because of *me*!"

"Hey," she said throwing her hands up. "At least your ass isn't in jail."

I threw my face into my hands. "This shit is not cool. It's just not cool! King was supposed to be driving that night."

"And he wasn't. And Kennedy refused to turn him in. So..." She ended her comment with a shrug. But it wasn't that easy. The shit just wasn't over like that. How was I supposed to continue my relationships with my crew knowing that I was the cause of its heartbreak? Then my phone rang and Elijah's picture popped up. That was when I realized how I was going to move on with life. I had been undoubtedly more loyal to King than anyone in his life, so much so that I had kept every one of his trifling, dirty secrets. And I had kept the biggest secret of all, which was his son. I had even kept the secret from him so that he could enjoy his fucking marriage! I knew that if I told King about my baby, he would've tried to force me to have an abortion. And then, if I'd had my baby anyway, I would've ruined King's happily ever after. So I had sacrificed my child having a relationship with his father for King.

I had sacrificed my own son's happiness so that nigga could be happy because I loved him that much. Nobody loved him as much as I did. Not those random ass bitches he was fucking with. Not Tiana. And not even Kennedy. She felt like she had made a sacrifice that day, but she hadn't made the biggest because her and her child would still have King at the end of the day. Me and my son didn't! I had watched him move mountains for Kayla, when he didn't even look at my son long enough to see himself in Elijah's walk, talk, and laughter.

Detective Sanchez noticed my demeanor changing. She noticed that I was no longer upset about what had taken place that day. "You cool?"

I ran my fingers through my weave and adjusted my purse on my shoulders. "Yeah, I'm more than cool."

"Good. That girl will be alright. She got years, but she is only required to do half. Four years won't kill her."

NOVEMBER 2012

CHAPTER NINETEEN

KENNEDY

On November 10, 2012, I turned myself in to the authorities. It was the saddest day of my life. Imagine attending your own funeral. That's how it felt.

King and I had spent the morning making love. He touched my body like he never had before, like it was the last time because it undoubtedly would be the last time for a long time. Our orgasms were accompanied with tears, and then, with shaky legs still quaking from King's touch, I went into Kayla's room, scooped her out of her crib, and brought her back in the bed with me and King. We all spooned together until I was forced to shower and go to the county.

Jada, Dolla, Meech, Siren, and my mother had all met us at the house before we left. They tailed me, King and Kayla. As we arrived at the county, I truly felt like King's queen, arriving with my court in tow.

I held Kayla for as long as I could. As they all hugged me and said their goodbyes, I held Kayla close to my chest, only letting her go and handing her to Jada when it was time for me to say goodbye to King.

"Help King with Kayla, okay?" I told Jada as she took my daughter from my arms.

Through tears, she sucked her teeth, saying, "Girl, you know I got you."

I took a deep breath, looked at King and buried myself into him. We had cried all of our tears out that morning. His eyes were dry but dreary and lifeless as we held each other for dear life.

I could hear Mr. Thomas calling my name from the stairs of the building. It was time for me to go. I reluctantly let King go, but he continued holding me until the very last moment. When his eyes found mine, I smiled into them to give him strength, to give *us* strength.

But I fell into his arms again. I couldn't help it. I just needed one more touch to take with me, to imagine how his arms felt around me as I slept alone at night. He wrapped his arms around me tighter than he ever had before. I wished that I could stay in his arms forever, but I had made this choice, and it was the right choice. So I was actually ready to do what I had to do.

"I love you," he whispered into my ear.

I smiled, mentally bookmarking this moment so that those words could replay with the feelings of his lips against my ears for the next four years. "How much?"

When his chest heaved, and I heard him sigh, my heart broke for him. I sympathized with him more than I did for my mother. But I knew that I had sacrificed for the right man when he said his ritual, "More than anything."

"I love you too," I told him, as I forced back tears.

"How much?"

And a genuine chuckle left my throat when I answered, "More than Kanye loves Kanye."

Present day

Five days after release

CHAPTER TWENTY

KENNEDY

I took a deep breath as I killed the engine. "Okay, Kayla. Let's do this."

She actually sucked her teeth. "Do what?"

I shook my head with a chuckle. "I want you to meet your granddaddy."

I could hear her saying something that I couldn't make out as I climbed out of the car with wobbly legs. I was so nervous to ring that doorbell, especially since I hadn't even bothered to let him know that I was coming. But he hadn't answered my calls in five years, not even while I was in prison, so I assumed that he wouldn't answer now.

I wondered if my father would even answer the door, but I was willing to take the risk. Being home these past few days had been a dream come true, but seeing my father would make it all the better.

While I was prison, I wanted nothing more than to at least see my father's face again. So as I got Kayla out of her car seat, I told myself that if he at least opened the door and let me stare into his eyes, I would be happy with that, even if he slammed the door in my face afterward.

Walking up the driveway while holding Kayla's hand was an eerie, unsettling feeling. I had become exactly what my father didn't want me to be: a failure. In his eyes, as well as my own, I hadn't accomplished the goals in life that I'd held closest to my heart. But as I felt the warmth of my hand, I knew I had accomplished a lot more than the average woman and exactly what many of them dreamed of. I was a wife and mother, and although the last few years had been weary, I was proud to say that I was dedicated to both Kayla and King. As I rang the doorbell, I hoped that my father would at least see how I unconditionally loved them both and how that love overshadowed every fucked up thing that had happened to me in my life. That love made everything worth it.

I could hear shuffling on the other side off the door, and my knees shook violently. I caught a glimpse of him through the red curtains that still covered the door panel. Just seeing his shadow made me emotionally full. Tears came to my eyes and a small moan escaped my throat loud enough for Kayla to hear. She looked up at me with her thick, luscious eyebrows curled tightly with confusion. "What's wrong wit'chu?"

I chuckled, finally feeling some sense of happiness because, after five years, I would be in the arms of the only man that I loved just as much as King. But seconds crept by, and then nearly a minute of no further sounds or movement. I could imagine that I looked just like Kayla when I curled my eyebrows just as tightly and rang the doorbell again. I knew he was on the other side of that door. I could feel it and I could feel him.

"Daddy?" I called out as I rang the bell. Then my heart began to flutter as anticipation returned when I could hear the shuffling on the other side of the door again. But my heart sank as I realized that the sounds were getting fainter and fainter.

Through the door panel, I saw my daddy. Even only looking at the back of him, I could see how he had aged. He no longer stood tall and proud. His walk was slow. His hair was longer. My heart sank as I wondered if I had done so much wrong that I had aged him, if I had made him such a mean old man that he would walk away from me as I stood on the other side of the door yearning for him. But I didn't need to wonder. I forced back tears as I began to lead Kayla away from the door. I knew that I had.

"Where we goin'?" Kayla asked curiously.

I grimaced as I answered, "We're going home, baby."

"But I t'ought I was gon' see my gran-daddy?"

A deep sigh responded to her before I could. "Not today, baby...not today."

This time when she sucked her teeth, I actually didn't mind, because I felt the same frustration. I had been so hopeful during the drive to the Thornridge, but I was walking in my reality as I approached the driveway. I should have known better than to anticipate that that stubborn old man would change his ways just because I had once again tried to fix it.

But anticipation returned quickly as I heard the faint sounds of the latches of a door moving. I quickly turned around, my heart barely beating with hope.

"Kennedy?"

As soon as I heard his voice, I jogged up the pathway of the house that had turned me into the loyal woman that I was, dragging poor Kayla along with me. I ran toward the man that had taught me everything. As soon as I passed the shrubs and came upon the doorway, he was stepping out with wide eyes, wondering if I'd left.

I ran to him. His arms weren't open to embrace me when I engulfed him in mine, but I didn't care. I had let go of Kayla and hugged him so tight that I knew that I was hurting him.

"I'm sorry," I cried. "I'm so sorry, daddy."

He wasn't saying anything. He wasn't hugging me, and that was okay. I just kept hugging him and apologizing while enjoying the feeling of him back in my arms. For so long I thought that I didn't need him. I had acted like I didn't care. But the moment that he finally wrapped his arms around me, I truly felt like I was no longer imprisoned. Relief left my body in uncontrollable gasps and sobs, and I nearly fainted when he kissed my cheek, saying, "I'm sorry too."

SIREN

Meech had kicked me out of the house with nothing. I didn't have a cell phone, a purse, or even a wallet. All I was wearing was the leggings, sports bra and flip flops that I had been lounging around the house in. I was walking down the main street near our community, on my way to the lounge that Meech and I frequented. I was cool with the bartenders and owners, so I figured that I could use one of their phones to call my mom or get a ride to the city.

"Siren!"

My eyes rolled into the back of my head as soon as I heard her irritating, Latin accent.

"Not now!" I screeched over my shoulder. "I don't feel like your shit today!"

I could hear the engine of her car turning off.

"Urgh. Now I gotta deal with this bitch," I muttered under my breath as I slowed my pace. I hated to even be bothered with her, but at the moment I needed a friend, and after all these years, Detective Sanchez had become a friend. It's easy for two people from two different paths to become friends when they have the same enemy.

Plus, I figured she could give me a ride.

I could hear the heels of her shoes against the pavement, so I turned around reluctantly. I wasn't worried about Meech seeing me because he looked like he never wanted to see my ass again, so him coming to look for me was out of the fucking question.

"What's up, Maria?" At this point, me and Detective Sanchez were on a first name basis.

She walked toward me with a half-smile. "What are you doing walking out here? And why aren't you answering your phone?"

"I don't have my fucking phone." Then I sighed, revealing, "Meech kicked me out."

She chuckled, "Damn."

"Fuck you, Maria. This isn't funny." We had a bit of a love-hate relationship. "What do you want?"

"Pieces of Lock's body have been found in an alley in the city. I know he's done some work for King's crew in the past. You hear anything about a murder? Maybe they thought Lock was the snitch that was leading us to them regarding Terry's murder?"

I shrugged my shoulders with irritation. "I don't know, Maria."

Her head cocked to the side, causing her authentic red curls to fall in her eyes. "You sure about that?"

"Hell yeah, I'm sure!" I snapped, smacking my lips.

"C'mon, Siren. I know you have more than that."

"I don't! Look, I have given you all that I can. What else do you want me to do?"

I had. After being the cause of Kennedy's arrest, I felt guilty as fuck, but that only lasted for a few months. Over time, the guilt subsided, and my love-hate relationship with King once again took over. I wanted that nigga gone, but I wanted him with me at the same time. So, after Kennedy was locked up for a while, I tried my luck. A year after Kennedy had been locked up, King was still a shell of the person he once was. He had lost weight, he was unusually quiet, and he stayed to himself. All he could think about was his hustle and Kayla. I figured that he was dying for the love and affection of someone familiar, and although I was his best friend's woman, I figured that he would remember the nights that I had taken care of him and his needs. But once again, he shut me down cold, looking at me like I was so unworthy of being with the "infamous King."

His rejection only fueled my obsession. I was angry that he didn't see in me what he had seen in so many other bitches. Every time I wondered what was better about a bitch in prison than me standing in front of him with an eager, wet and ready mouth and pussy, my anger grew. Who the fuck did he think he was? A king, that's what! That nigga really thought he was some fucking royalty, and apparently I was a peasant. Then when Kennedy got out and he acted like the fucking Queen of England was arriving in the Chi, my love turned to pure hate once again. I called Maria and told her about the night that Meech came home drunk and talking loudly on the phone. It was the day before Kennedy's return. I was lying on the couch, pretending to be sleep, as I waited for him to come home from handling some business with Dolla. He was in the kitchen when I heard him say, "We might have to handle that nigga like we did Terry, in broad daylight in front of his family. Then he'll know not to fuck with us."

Everybody in the hood figured that someone in King's crew was responsible for Terry's murder in retaliation for setting up Rozay. But of course, no one cared or snitched because they figured Terry deserved it for even attempting to come against the infamous King and his crew. But I was more than ready to come against him as I watched King literally praise Kennedy's ass as he prepared for her to come home. The sacrifice that she had made had gained her so much undying loyalty from him. The nigga hadn't even touched a piece of pussy in the time that she was gone. She made one fucking heroic move and she was a saint in his eyes, but everything that I had done was overlooked. So the morning of Kennedy's return, I called Maria and told her about what I'd heard Meech say and the van that I'd seen them all climb into a few hours before Terry's murder. I knew that this information would most likely lead to Dolla and Meech's arrest as well, and the demise of their entire empire, but I didn't give a fuck, as long as King was rotting in jail.

It just wasn't fair! He was so happy, walking around like he didn't have a care in the world, especially not for me, when my heart ached every time my son asked for his father.

I just wanted him to hurt like I had been for years.

"Just go arrest his ass," I spat with a frown. Just thinking of him irritated my soul. Everything was his fault. My constant unhappiness was his fault because nothing made me happy because I wasn't with him, not even Meech. Even at that moment, as I stood now without a home, it was all King's fault because my dumbass was protecting him while I lied to everyone about who Elijah's father was.

"I want to!" Maria responded. "That slick motherfucker is airtight. None of my evidence against him will hold up in court."

"Well, what the fuck else you want me to do?"

"Testify against him."

"Are you crazy?!" I asked, with a possessed chuckle.

Maria came toward me with a look of desperation. "Your testimony will put him away for good."

I hated King, but I liked living. "I can't, Maria."

"Then I'll use what I have to arrest Meech," she threatened.

That was always her stronghold over me. She always threatened me with arresting Meech every time her bipolar ass came around with a new obsession with locking King up. But as the years went by, there was rarely anything that I could give her. I was Meech's woman, so my involvement in the business became less and less. He rarely told me anything and telling her about any drops that me and Jada did weren't an option because I wasn't about to send me or her to jail. I had nothing until I overheard Meech's drunk talk about Terry's murder.

"That ain't gon' work this time," I muttered as I waved my hand dismissively. "That nigga don't want me no more. He just literally put me out on the street. Do what you gotta do."

Maria looked at me like she was disappointed with my defeated spirit. "Come on, Siren. I'll give you a ride. Where are you..."

My attention went away from Maria as I looked up the street.

"Get out of here!" I spat as I noticed Jada's Range Rover coming our way.

Maria looked at me like I was crazy as I began to speed walk away from her. "What's—"

"Go!" I spat over my shoulder. "Just go!"

Then I heard Jada's familiar voice, "Siren! Siren, come here."

JADA

Nah, don't walk away now, bitch. I had been parked on the corner watching Siren talk to this detective for ten damn minutes! *What the fuck was she doing talking to a detective?* I thought as I watched them talk like they were the best of friends. It was apparent that they knew each other and knew each other well.

Meech had called and asked me to come find Siren. He'd told me that they got into it, and he kicked her out with nothing, but he wouldn't tell me what they'd gotten into it about when I asked. Of course, I got right up, threw some clothes on, and came looking for my girl. Imagine my surprise when I peeped her in a deep conversation with the police. She was in plain clothes, but I knew a detective whenever I saw one.

As soon as I started to pull up, Siren peeped me and nearly ran away from the bitch. Finally, when I began to call her name, the female detective walked away, hopped in her unmarked car, and sped off.

I called her name again, "Siren!" Finally, the heifer turned around like she had just heard me.

She looked at me and sighed with relief. "Jada, thank God! I'm so happy to see you, girl." She actually rushed toward my truck and opened the door, ignoring the confused snarl on my face. "What are you doing on this side of town?"

"Meech called me and told me to come looking for you."

A look of relief came over her. "For real? What did he say?"

"He said that y'all got into it–"

"Did he tell you why?" she asked, cutting me off with a frightened look.

"Naaah…" I spoke slowly because all of this was really throwing me off. She was acting like I didn't just see her talking to a detective and was scared as fuck that Meech had told me what their argument was about. "He just wanted me to come give you a ride."

"Oh." Then both relief and disappointment filled her eyes.

I slowly pulled off as anger started boiling inside of me. This had been my best friend, my bitch, for years. I knew her. There was no fucking way that she knew the police. She didn't have any friends in the department. And nobody that lived the life that we lived should have been talking to the police.

Siren looked at me curiously as I pulled my truck into the alley and then parked in the back of an apartment building. "Where are we going?"

I ignored her questioning glare and killed the engine. "What the fuck were you doing hollering at the police, Siren?"

First, she tried to play dumb. "Huh? What?"

"Don't play with me, Siren!" She was shocked, and so was I, when tears came to my eyes. I was asking her, but the answer was obvious to me. There was no reason for her to be cool with a detective without me knowing unless she was on some snake shit. "I know you, bitch. I know your life. You haven't told me about having no friends in the department, but I watched you holding a conversation with this bitch. So who the fuck is she?"

Siren stared blankly out of the window as tears filled her eyes. "I don't know her. Now would you c'mon? Drive! Shit!"

I bit my lip so hard that I could damn near taste blood. "Siren, don't fucking play with me."

"I'm not!"

"You gon' sit here and lie to me?"

"I'm not–"

"Fuck that shit, Siren! Tell me the truth!"

Siren knew about Terry's murder. Although I didn't tell that to Dolla the other day, I knew that Siren had overheard Meech talking about the murder. She'd secretly told me as we got massages the day that Kennedy got out. But even when Dolla told me that he had been questioned, I never even considered that it was Siren; not my girl, not my best friend, not my *family*.

She looked at me like I was the one that was crazy. "Ain't shit to tell!" she shrieked.

I glared back at her, never backing down. "So you ain't the one that snitched?"

Before she even knew what she was doing, she looked at me with bulging eyes, as if she was wondering how I knew, but she quickly fixed her face. "What the fuck are you talking about?"

Apparently, Meech hadn't been as honest with her about what was going on as Dolla had been with me. But still I knew it was her. Seeing her talk to that bitch cop, it all made sense.

299

My heart broke and tears filled my eyes once again. "It *was* you, wasn't it?"

Siren sucked her teeth and waved her hand. "I don't know what the fuck you talkin' about?"

"Really, Siren? You just gon' sit there and play stupid? How could you? Kennedy just got out and–"

"Fuck Kennedy! Fuck King!" She had become so possessed with anger that she didn't even realize it. She looked disgusted as she ranted and raved. "Fuck them, damn! Who gives a fuck?"

I sat back, looking at her with disgust. "Apparently, you do."

Siren finally looked me in my eyes and saw that I was reading her like a book. She thought she had been slick all of these years, but I could see that she was crushing on King, and I could see her jealously when he got with Tiana and then Kennedy. And jealousy will make you do some foul shit. "You're a fucking snitch," I said as I shook my head. "I can't believe this shit."

"You know what? Fuck this!" she snapped as she grabbed the door handle. "I ain't gotta listen to this bullshit! I'll walk!"

As she climbed out of the car, so did I. I jumped out and was about to catch up with her just as she made it to the alley. But she wasn't able to take another step before I snatched my piece from my waist, aimed at her back and pulled the trigger. The popping sound piercing the air made her jump, but she soon hit the ground. Before she could even figure out what was happening to her, I was standing over her. I closed my eyes with regret before aiming at her head and pulling the trigger. I couldn't even watch as I killed my best friend, but as I turned and ran away from her bleeding and dying body, I knew it was what had to be done. I loved her like a sister, but she had come against others that I loved, and nobody came against my family.

****

I cried the entire way home. It hurt my heart that Siren was gone and that I would never hear her laugh again. I would never be able to gossip with her again, but I felt no guilt that I was the one that had taken her away from me.

"Baby? What's wrong?!"

I had come into the house with tears streaming down my face. Dolla dropped the X-box controller and immediately ran toward me as I closed the door. I fell into his arms and sobbed aloud as I held him tightly.

"Bae, please talk to me," he begged, as he kissed the top of my head. "What's wrong?"

"It was Siren!" I cried.

"What? What was Siren?"

I breathed in deeply and attempted to stop my tears. I knew that I had to get it together in order to tell Dolla everything. And I did. I let him go, wiped my face and walked toward the couch with him on my heels. I was still shaking as he sat closely beside me and held my hand.

"When I went looking for Siren, I found her standing on the street talking to a detective. She was in plain clothes, but I peeped the unmarked car. She was a Latino, redhead, just like the bitch that you said pulled you over the other day." Tears still silently slid down my face as I recalled the moments that I knew I would never forget. "I pulled over at the corner and watched her have this deep as discussion with this chick. When I couldn't take it anymore, I pulled off and drove toward her. When she saw me, she hit it one way, and the detective hit it in another. I knew something was up. Siren got in my car like nothing had even happened." I shook my head, still disappointed in her. "I asked her what she was doing talking to her and she played dumb. It was obvious right then! Baby, she knew about Terry's murder–"

"No, she didn't. Meech said he–"

"Meech never told her, but she overheard him talking about it a few days ago."

His eyes bucked. "Why didn't you tell me?!"

"I told Siren I wouldn't! I'm sorry!" I cried.

Dolla shook his head in disbelief. "Why would she snitch? Bae, I don't think Siren would do that."

"She had to. She overheard Meech talking and then the police show up the next day questioning you? That shit ain't no coincidence! We were there that day when y'all left. We saw y'all in the van, remember?"

It took Dolla a few minutes to take it all in, but when he did and realized the truth, his face fell in his hands as his head shook with regret.

"That bitch has been lying to me! To *me*, her best fucking friend. And then she snitched on my nigga! On Meech and King! On my family! How could she?" I shook my head, the heartbreak causing a pain that I had never felt before.

"Why the fuck would she snitch?"

I sucked my teeth. "She kept acting like I didn't know what I was talking about, but that bitch was lying! I could tell."

Dolla looked into the air with disappointment. It finally all made sense to him too. Siren was a snitch. "So what's gon' stop her from telling some other shit?"

Tears filled my eyes again as I admitted, "She's not going to say anything else because I...killed her."

I didn't even see Dolla's reaction because I threw my face into my hands and began to sob. I could feel his arms wrapped tightly around me as his phone rang. He continued holding me as he answered, "What up, Meech?"

I instantly sat up and shot bulging eyes at Dolla as I heard Meech ask, "Aye, bruh, did Jada get back? She ain't answerin' her phone."

"Yeah, she back. She's in the shower."

"Did she find Siren?"

"Nah, man. I was just about to call you. She said she didn't see her."

"Oh…a'ight then."

"Call her mama's house. Maybe she got a ride there."

"Nah, it's all good. I don't care that much. Fuck that bitch."

"Damn, bruh. It's like that? What happened?"

I could tell that Dolla and I were thinking the same thing. Did they get into it because Meech had also found out that Siren was a snitch?

But he only answered, "Some bullshit, bruh. I just can't trust her ass."

"That's fucked up."

"Ain't it?" he sighed. "Well, I'll holla at you tomorrow."

"A'ight, bruh. One."

As Dolla hung up, there was an eerie feeling in the air.

"You think he found out what she did?" I asked Dolla.

"Nah, he would have told me."

"What if the police have evidence, Dolla?" I started to freak. "What if they pin this shit on y'all?"

"Nah, it's all good. Whatever she told them wasn't shit. If it was, they would have arrested us. I'm sure they were trying to get some more evidence out of her but… you took care of that."

Once again, I began to sob into my hands. I was hurt that my friend, my *best* friend, had turned against us. I was confused because I'd had no idea why. I wanted to die because now she was gone, and it was because of me.

But Dolla wrapped his arms around me and held me again, assuring me. "You did what you had to do baby. You protected your family. And I'll protect you *forever*. No one will ever know."

KENNEDY

♪Can we stay home tonight?
Try something new tonight?
This drink got me feelin' right
I'm 'bout to lose my mind
U, Me, & Hennessy, look what you did to me
Fuckin' so crazy, you twirlin' and spinnin' me
My head keep on spinnin', my legs keep on shakin'
But my head keep on spinnin'
I'm out of my mind let's keep on sippin'
Let's make some babies, and make it official♪

King was in such a good mood that he stayed at home with Kayla and me all day, which I enjoyed. Whatever "business" that was taking him away from home, when I had imagined spending days after my release in his arms and never coming up for air, was finally "handled," so he said. So that day, I finally got what I had been waiting for: him. After returning from my father's house, we watched movies, laughed, reminisced, and fantasized about Cabo while Kayla ran rampant and didn't listen to a gawd damn thing I said.

Now, King and I were soaking in the Jacuzzi in our master bathroom. Finally, after a day of acting a whole damn fool, Kayla was asleep. King had awarded my Kayla Survival with Remy 1738 and his hands massaging my shoulders as I lay against his chest sipping and listening to the surround sound as the stars winked at me through the picture window.

"Sooo..." I smiled as I waited for King to continue. I knew that there was something to look forward to after that pause. "I have a surprise for you."

"What now, King?" Don't get me wrong. Surprises are always fun, but King had been suffocating me with gifts since my release. It had only been five days since I got home, and yet I had more clothes, shoes, jewelry, and trinkets than any woman could ask for.

"I'm throwing you a party for your birthday."

My face scrunched as I sipped from my glass. "But I just had a party. People are going to get tired of partying with me."

"But–"

I interrupted, "I just want to spend my birthday with you and Kayla before we leave for Cabo the next day. That's all I want."

"But it's an important party."

I sat up in the tub and turned toward him. That sneaky ass grin on his face said that he was up to a bunch of something.

"What kind of important party, King?"

He licked his lips as he smiled. I swear, I wanted to suck his dick right then. Just wanted to dive under that water and put his dick in my mouth!

He reached for me and brought me toward him. The water splashed and spilled onto the floor as we adjusted against one another. "It's our wedding."

"What?!" I whispered my shock. I was surprised, but not so much that I wanted to wake up Kayla's crazy ass!

He chuckled with his answer, "I said it's *our wedding*. That's your birthday party. "

"Oh my God, King!" My hands flew to my mouth, and, as they did, warm water splashed in our faces. We giggled, and he wiped his face as he replied, "I mean, we can't go to a honeymoon without having an official wedding. Right?"

I couldn't even answer. Staring into those loyal, adorable, romantic eyes of his, I fell in love all over again. I committed myself to him all over again. I even knew that if, God forbid, I had to, I would make the same sacrifices for him and my mean ass daughter all over again. I just leaned over and took the man's tongue into my mouth and breathed a sigh of relief.

For three years, I imagined how good it would feel to be home, but this was a feeling that I could not have imagined, not even in my wildest dreams.

♪ *Me, Hennessy & U*
Me, Hennessy & U
Me, Hennessy & U
Me, Hennessy & U
U, Me & Hennessy, look what you did to me
I say my head keep on spinnin'
Me, Hennessy & U ♪

A Thug's Love 2
Sneak Peek

CHAPTER ONE

JADA

Dolla held me until I stopped crying. That was for about two hours. Visions of Siren's life leaving her body in leaking crimson blood would not leave my mind and kept me crying out in agony and guilt. I felt like the lowest of the low. Sure, snitches get stitches. Siren deserved every bullet that I put in her. Yet, I hated that her killer ended up being me. I was so hurt by that because I had prided myself in being loyal to my family and friends. Yet, I had just killed my sister, my best friend.

Luckily, Dolla had allowed the kids to go down the street to play with friends, so I was free to moan, scream and cry out as much as I wanted... until my cell phone began to ring.

Initially, I ignored the call as my cell sat on the coffee table. It was a number that wasn't saved in my contacts. Current matters left me too scared to answer the phone for anyone that I did not know. But when the caller continued to call back to back, I left Dolla's arms, disguised my tears, and answered, "Who is this?"

"Hello?" The caller was taken aback by my attitude and it showed in her shaky, yet professional tone. "May I speak to Jada Davenport, please?"

I ignored the noises in her background and the sincerity in her tone. I was too engulfed in my own worry and turmoil to even think to pay attention. I just, again, gave her an attitude. I sucked my teeth and blew heavy breath in frustration. "Who the fuck is this?"

Dolla looked at me curiously, as his concern begin to grow the longer I held the phone to my ear.

The female caller stumbled over her words as she tried to talk around my obvious irate attitude. "I-I'm a nurse at Saint Mary's Medical Center. Your name was given as an emergency contact for Siren Green. Ma'am..." Her pause was full of concern as her words came out full of compassion, while I attempted to fight the urge to completely lose it when she said Siren's name. "Siren was ...shot... a few hours ago. She's in surgery. You should come down right away."

Surgery? I thought as my eyes darted towards Dolla's, wide with unease. "Shot?" I questioned the caller, my voice shaking with what she thought was fear for my friend, but was actually fear for myself. "Surgery? So that means she's still alive? Sh-she survived?"

I saw the color leave Dolla's brown skin as I could regretfully hear the smile in the caller's words. "Yes, she survived. I'm sure she'll pull through surgery just fine, ma'am. But please do come right away."

to be continued...

Text the keyword "Jessica" to 25827 to receive text message alerts of future releases from Jessica N. Watkins.

JESSICA'S CONTACT INFO:

Amazon page: http://ow.ly/LYLEL

Facebook: http://www.facebook.com/authorjwatkins

Facebook group:
http://www.facebook.com/groups/femistryfans

Twitter: @authorjwatkins

Instagram: @authorjwatkins

Email: jessica.n_watkins@yahoo.com

Made in the USA
Middletown, DE
10 April 2017